Feathered Dreams

Book 1

By: Brittany Putzer

Feathered Dreams

Dedication

To Karen: who I "maid that smells so goo" (inside pre-editing joke). And to God who gave me the imagination to conjure this book series. Also, to my lovely family who I couldn't have done this without. Love you Charlie, Charles, Paul, Melody, Becky, Alicia, Kathie, Daddy, Hannah, Biena and all my furry, feathered, scaled, and non-furry companions that help me through this mundane life. I wish I could list you all, but you know who you are! Your love has helped me soar through this publishing process with grace (and a few tears). I will be forever grateful for your support.

#PutzerReadingTribe

Contents

Feathered Beginnings

The dark storm builds overhead as thunder booms in the distance. I sigh as I swipe my dirt-covered hand across my face. Sharp twigs dig into my knees as I kneel in the grass, glaring into the bush. This has to stop. I don't know how much longer I can do this.

"Pecker, if you don't get out of there right now, I will be forced to use drastic measures." I glare at her as sweat inches towards my eyes, but I don't back down. "One, two, two and a half, two and three quarters. Pecker. Don't make me get to three. Fine, let's do this the hard way." I groan as I climb into the shrubbery, ignoring spider webs, thorns, and poison ivy to grab the black-and-white hen who insisted on making a nest in these stupid bushes right before bedtime. As I feel the fluff of her spoiled butt, I hear a gasp.

"Ann, what are you doing in the dirt? Your date will be here any minute and you look like you've been rolling in the pigpen."

I back out with Pecker screeching and flapping spastically, causing red scratches across my cheek. "Dad, I'm sorry. Pecker got stuck in the bushes and the coyotes could have attacked her." I try my best to appear innocent, as I go towards him holding out the evidence. But my dad shakes his head while he pulls out a twig and feather from my messy braid.

Pecker struggles in my tight grip. I stroke her soft feathers and think to myself: *I did it again.* That look dad gave

1

me. I know he wants me to be happy. And in his mind, that means going out, dating, and marrying one day. But I disappoint him.

"Dad, I'm sorry. Really I am."

"You said that last time, Ann, remember? The white chicken in the tree? You nearly broke your neck grabbing that hen."

"Fluffy went up there and I couldn't let a hawk attack her." I march Pecker to her pen and toss her in with a warning look. "We will talk about this later."

I slam the pen door shut. Running inside, I kick off my muddy boots and black sludge speckles the floor. I hear the doorbell. My head shoots up. My shirt is muddy, and my pants are splattered in—*don't ask.* I facepalm and drag my feet to open the door.

My date is staring at my disarray with wide eyes. Jim is an old high school acquaintance. He was charming and sweet but has not worked a day in his life. I force a smile and ignore his open mouth.

"Uh, am I early?"

"Sorry, Jim, I was rescuing Pecker from a bush and I lost track of time."

"Pecker... and a bush—okay. Ann, I don't think this is going to work." He walks away to his red sports car, shaking his head and not looking back at my defeated form.

I shout after him, trying to explain, but that only makes him move faster. He gets into his car and drives off with a squeal of high-performance tires. As gravel flies all around me, I sigh at my bootless feet. Twenty-one years old and I haven't had a serious boyfriend. Well, unless I can count holding hands with Richard in middle school.

As the red dot disappears into the distance, I'm stopped by our neighbor, Suzie. She is a pleasant, older divorced woman, but she tends to stick her nose in our business. "Ann, you are an absolute mess. Was that your date leaving?"

I try not to roll my eyes at her observation. My mom died from cancer when I was ten-years old, and since then Suzie has been inserting herself into my life like the replacement I never wanted. Although she is kind and honest, I am not that little girl. I force a smile as I brush past her.

"Your dad made you a deal. If you start dating, you don't have to put your name in for the Prince."

I purse my lips, feeling my face flush. *There it is.* The real reason she is prodding me about my dating life. The stupid semi-arranged wedding for the Monarchy. When the firstborn becomes twenty-one, he or she must pick a commoner to be their spouse. This tradition gives every state a chance to present their favorite women or men for the opportunity to marry a future ruler. It allows the people's voice to be heard. It's been a custom in our country for centuries, but I have no interest in it. I don't want to live in a palace, wear expensive dresses, or be forced to be proper. And

I don't want to be pushed to marry somebody I don't like just because it's the social norm.

No, thank you.

I love my life as it is, chickens and all, but I understand my dad's interest. Whoever wins—or loses depending on how you look at it—gets a nice paycheck for as long as they are away from their family. The money could really help the farm. And then I can find true love and he can die happy. It's a fairy-tale ending.

"Yes, Ms. Suzie, I know the arrangement, but Dad understands that I have responsibilities and things happen that I can't control. There will be plenty of time to set up another date."

That night I have a quiet dinner of hotdogs with macaroni and cheese. I eat with Dad, and afterwards, we sit in the living room to relax. Dad turns the television up as we settle into our nighttime routine. I brush my hair after my shower, while grabbing a favorite book off my shelf. I rub my hand over the worn spine and turn to my favorite chapter. I put my feet up in my recliner, trying my best to ignore the news. There's never anything good to report: it's either negative or boring. It seems pointless to me, or it does until I hear my name mentioned and, out of the corner of my eye, I see my picture flash on the screen. My book slips from my fingertips and crashes onto the floor. I stare at the TV and hear the end of the segment.

"And this is the lineup of the lucky girls nominated for the opportunity to marry our Prince. Congratulations, ladies."

If I could give a death glare or die of embarrassment, this would be the time. As my face turns red, I stare at my dad. "Dad. Tell me you didn't sign me up for that ridiculous competition."

"A deal is a deal, young lady."

They called my name. I run a hand through my hair and pull, as my eyes lose focus. I'm legally obligated to go to the Palace with a flock of other women to compete in winning the Prince's heart.

This can't be happening.

Hiding out and ignoring the Palace phone calls works for a day or two, but I can't ignore them forever. They won't let me. Representatives from the Royal Family come in like a hurricane and take over my quiet farming life. Tutors arrive and teach me how to walk in heels, eat, and even how to speak properly. My dad is beside himself seeing me in dresses and learning manners. I am not; it's a nightmare. I want to snitch on my dad for putting my application through, but I don't want to get him into trouble. I do as much as I can around the farm, between training sessions, and leave Dad a list of to-dos and places to check at night in case Pecker or Fluffy get any crazy ideas of breaking out again.

Before I know it, it's the morning of the competition and time for me to say my goodbyes to everybody. Dad hugs me tight and whispers, "Ann, honey, please don't be mad at me. Who knows? You may even enjoy yourself. The worst-case scenario is that nothing comes of it and then you'll be home in a few weeks, right?"

I can't stay mad at him because he only wants the best for me. But it reminds me how little he knows me and what I want for my life. I kiss his cheek and it takes everything for me to walk away from our home.

The four-hour drive is quiet as I watch out of the dark-tinted window. I try not to cry as my hometown passes in a blur. As a distraction, I rummage through my bag. I packed comfortable clothes for the ride and some essentials, but I'm surprised to see a few odds and ends that I didn't put in there. I tilt my head and smirk as I pull out a stuffed animal; it's a chicken that almost looks like Whitey with its red comb and white feathers. I start laughing. Then tears fall as I hold the soft toy close to my heart. I hear a crinkle and find a handwritten letter from my dad.

Ann,

I can't imagine how hard this must be for you, because for me, it's like a piece of my soul is being torn out. After your mother died, you had a lot of roles to fill. And you did an amazing job. But it is time for you to fly the coop—see, I can be funny too. You need to see what the world has to offer you and you to it. I feel I have held you back for far too long, Ann, my dear, so spread your wings. I know you will soar to some amazing heights. Remember I love you and only want the best for you. Please give this an honest try.

All my hugs,

Dad

Behind the letter is my old camera. I took a digital photography course one summer and loved it so much that Dad bought me this camera the following Christmas. I push the power button and scroll through the images. The memories flood my mind. What I wouldn't give to go back to simpler days. Setting the camera back into my bag, I stare ahead.

I smile at the driver in the rearview mirror.

"Anything I can do for you, Lady Ann?" His words pierce my ears like nails on a chalkboard. They warned me I'd have my new title of *Lady*. But I don't want to be known publicly for my gender.

"How long have you been with the palace, mister?"

"Ben, my lady. Since I was a boy. I started in the stables and worked my way up to this position."

I'm used to being busy all the time on the farm and sitting here makes me jittery. And if I stare out the window, I will get car sick. Which would be very embarrassing and not the greatest way to start out as a "lady." I consider playing twenty questions with Mr. Ben.

The ride goes well and Mr. Ben is easy to talk to. Especially since he comes from a humble background. We discuss the Palace horses and, to my utter excitement, their chickens. They're raised for meat, so the excitement doesn't last because the chickens don't have a long or happy life like my free-range egg-layers back home. I'm dismayed and it makes me miss my girls.

The four hours pass as Ben tells me about himself and the Palace way of life. I see the grand, looming structure in front of me. Mr. Ben opens my door and I freeze. I can't do this. "Are you okay, Lady Ann? You look pale. Should I go get the doctor?"

I'm being a coward. I grab his outstretched, work-worn hand and step into the warm sunlight. My eyes are assaulted by the sights around me. The bright sweet-smelling flowers, the white fountains, and all the shady trees are beautiful and well maintained.

"Thank you, Mr. Ben, but that won't be necessary."

He grabs my luggage and hands it to the staff members who flutter out of the palace like finches. I don't know where to stand or what to do. A well-dressed woman guides me in the right direction, but when we step through the massive front door, my jaw drops. It's magnificent. There are so many colors, hanging portraits, and paintings—my eyes don't know where to focus.

"Welcome to the Palace, Lady Ann." Her voice drones on, but I only catch the end of her instructions as she disappears around the corner.

I hear something about the first door on the first floor. But there are tons of doors. And, more specifically, one on each side of said first door. I peek my head inside the door on the left, ready to back out at a million miles an hour if there's somebody in there in a state of undress.

A grin spreads over my face as I stare at an enormous library. It's beautifully lit with huge windows drawing in the natural sunlight, while the sheer size offers various tables to sit. I finger some of the closest worn spines, relishing the familiar smell of old books as I twirl in the open space. I'm delighted and wonder if this might not be so bad after all. My eyes skip over a few of the titles and authors.

I'm in heaven.

"I have never seen such happiness over books." A man's deep voice comes from the back corner of the room. He is staring at my shocked expression with a novel in his hand. His soft brown eyes are lit with humor and a hint of disbelief.

My face pinkens at being caught dancing in a library. This man appears important, going by the way he's dressed in a light grey suit as well as the manner in which he speaks. I tilt my head as I watch him and try to cover my embarrassment with a smile. "The more that you read, the more things you will know. The more that you learn, the more places you'll go." I respond with an old quote from a book my mom used to read to me, hoping to spark his curiosity and test his intelligence.

The man blinks, trying to recall the quote, and pushes to his feet. Oh boy, he's taller than I thought. Tall, dark, and handsome. I feel my face flush as he closes his book with long fingers and sets it down. He comes within arm's reach and stops. As he towers over me, he stares into my hazel eyes as if he is trying to read my soul. "Interesting quote. Mark Twain?"

"No, it is not."

Somebody enters, breaking the silence with a gasp. "Lady Ann, you are supposed to be in the sitting room."

"My apologies, I got lost."

The well-dressed woman from earlier purses her lips at me. "Prince Ryan, I'm sorry. Forgive her. She is one of the new girls."

My head shoots from the woman to the Prince, who is smirking, before I'm quickly escorted to the sitting room — which is the first door on the right. Just as she said.

How could I be so naive as to not recognize the Prince? But I can't dwell on it because I am late to the gathering. As I enter the sitting room, the nine other participants turn towards me. I find a spot on one of the plush couches. The blonde-haired, blue-eyed girl next to me smiles.

"Good evening, my name is Lady Mary."

"It's nice to meet you, Lady Mary. My name is Ann."

"Nice to meet you, Lady Ann."

Everybody is gorgeous and I feel average. I run my hands over the soft yellow fabric in my lap, bite my lip, and push aside my insecurities, as the room is hushed and a beautiful woman enters.

She appears older, with long blonde hair and sharp icy eyes. Her gold dress sparkles in the light and her jeweled crown dazzles us. "Good afternoon, ladies. I am pleased to see you all here today. I am Queen Elizabeth. Welcome to our home. Over the next few weeks, my son will try to fall in love with one of you. And I will have gained a daughter."

We all giggle at her honesty.

She smiles as she continues. "Let's all join the rest of the family for dinner and then you may see your rooms, unpack, and settle in. Because tomorrow starts your new life."

She exits with grace and elegance, and the girls follow her to the dining room—which is adorned with red carpet and banners with gold lining. There are tables with silver name plates on top of white china, and we find our designated seats.

Once the King and Queen are seated, all heads turn to the back of the room as two young gentlemen walk in. One I recognize from the library as Prince Ryan, and to my surprise and amusement, he winks at me as he passes to sit with his parents. I blush and give an awkward nod before turning forward to face the front as they find their chairs.

The one I do not recognize addresses us. "Good evening and welcome to the Palace. My name is Prince Christian. I am honored to see you aiming to win the privilege of being my wife, and I look forward to meeting you all soon. I hope you feel welcome to explore our home—just please stay off the third floor."

He gives us a stern look.

As he speaks, I force a polite smile. Prince Christian is handsome with dirty-blonde hair, and muscles, but his piercing eyes are cold and distant. Prince Ryan is the opposite. He's calm with a hint of mischief in his brown eyes as he smirks at me and I smile back.

Dinner is too elegant for me to enjoy; the food is unfamiliar and I've never eaten squid in my life. However, the rice is flavorful with a hint of spice and that's decent enough. Dessert comes out and it looks fantastic. There's every flavor and color of macaroons you can imagine. I choose some blueberry ones.

Prince Ryan steps in front of me, and my heart skips a beat. I strive for something intelligent to say. "You still can't figure out the quote, can you?"

"Don't give up on me yet, Lady Ann. I may surprise you."

"I look forward to it, Prince Ryan."

He smirks. "Oh, so you do know my name?"

I try not to blush as he grabs a bright-red velvet macaroon and walks away. I watch him leave and find Lady Mary behind me. I jump as she says, "You know that's not the right Prince?" She is smiling as she teases me and grabs pink-colored peach macaroons.

"Thank you, Lady Mary. I'm aware of that, but Prince Christian doesn't seem short of ladies to talk to."

The man in question is surrounded by a gaggle of other participants, and we giggle at the sight. He hears us and glances over. We stop and smile while he continues to be mobbed, and we laugh again. When I've had my fill of macaroons, I go to my room to settle in.

As I'm wandering the corridor, I'm stopped by a young maid. "Good evening. Are you Lady Ann?"

"Yes, I am."

The woman beams at me in her starched black and white uniform, her dark eyes attentive. She appears to be my age without a single hair out of place. "I am your maid— Karen. May I show you to your room?"

My room is the size of two of my living rooms back home and has a massive queen bed, a shower, a bathtub, a walk-in closet filled with dresses and shoes, and a dresser. Though the most impressive feature is the giant window with French doors leading out to a private balcony. I run my hands over the soft bed cover as Karen unpacks my things and touches up the room. I push open the glass doors and walk into the crisp night air, feeling like a Princess.

And I breathe it in. It smells like home and I can't help the tears that roll down my face as I look around the yard. It's beautiful with green sculpted shrubs, towering trees, a water fountain, a small pond, and in the distance, I see a bright-red barn. I can almost make out the chicken coop and my heart aches to go visit my feathered friends.

As luxurious as it is, the Palace is no place for this farm girl. I cry in silence until something hits my arm. I ignore it but it happens again. Somebody is throwing something at me, but my eyesight is blurred from the tears, so I wipe the moisture away and frown at the ground below me.

Prince Ryan is throwing pebbles at the balcony. He waves me down. I squint at him and try to figure out what he is suggesting. He laughs and points a finger in my direction, then at the grass by him.

Karen is standing behind me laughing. "I think the Prince wants you to go down to meet him." She hesitates, her eyebrows knitted with concern. "Lady Ann, you've been crying. Are you all right?"

"I've never been away from my father before. I'm just homesick. Thank you, Karen. I better go see what Prince Ryan wants before he breaks the window with those rocks."

I was looking forward to being alone and being able to settle into my new environment, and by the time I get to the lawn, I'm annoyed by this sudden disturbance.

"Yes, my Prince?"

"And are you my Cinderella, Lady Ann?" His eyes flick to my bare feet.

I glance down and respond, "I doubt even Cinderella would wear heels like those."

He throws his head back and laughs. The sound is calming—it reminds me of the way my dad. We sit on a grey bench by the fountain. I put my toes in the cold water and the tiny colorful fish nibble them.

Prince Ryan clears his throat. "Lady Ann, are you all right? Why were you crying?"

"Have you ever worn heels before?"

"I can't say that I have. Although, I may be willing to try."

"How about a deal?"

"A deal? How intriguing. I am listening."

"I will tell you the author of that quote if you wear heels to breakfast."

"Lady Ann, I think that is against our dress code."

"Oh, live a little. You are a Prince. You can do what you want."

"Really? Well, then, I order you to tell me." The tone of his voice brings perspiration to my palms. When he cracks a smile, I relax.

"I'll gladly follow your order, *if* you're wearing heels in the morning."

"Rest well, Lady Ann."

"Good night, Prince Ryan."

I see the corners of his lips twitch as he shakes his head. I stand and smile into his dark eyes. I walk back to my room, feeling his curiosity linger on my departing figure. The pressure of a friendship seems far less intimidating than that of a relationship.

Trouble Begins

I was disappointed when I came down for breakfast and Ryan was not in heels.

I take my seat quietly and look around the room. Mary picks up on my frown and follows my stare. "Ann, need I remind you this is not the man you are looking for?"

"Mary, need I remind *you* that I know this." I pick up my coffee, breathe in the nutty aroma, and sigh happily.

She sticks her tongue out at me and I choke. I feel the liquid squirt from my nose. I squeal in protest as it burns. Then she laughs, choking on her eggs. As we clean ourselves, we see Prince Christian assessing us. "What is going on over here, ladies?"

"Prince Christian, I am sorry. We were just giddy." Mary blushes.

"We were laughing and got carried away." I smile up at him.

"And what about last night at dinner?"

"We like to laugh and have fun." I shrug.

"Even if it is at an inappropriate time and you cause a disruption? Do you like everyone staring at you? Are you that desperate for attention?" He crosses his arms over his chest and gives every impression of a pompous know-it-all.

My mouth drops open and closes, as he walks away shaking his head. I turn to Mary and watch tears stream down her beautifully painted face. "Oh, no. Lady Mary, don't cry.

We got carried away, but we did nothing wrong. Don't let Prince Christian get to you."

I hand her a napkin and she gets up and walks out of the room, leaving me behind, with everybody in the room staring at me. I send a glare towards Prince Christian's departing back. I grumble my way through the rest of breakfast, and afterwards I find most of the girls in the sitting room gossiping about the morning's events. I don't want to make small talk and I pretend not to notice the way the chatter stops when I hover in the doorway.

I decide to check on Mary. When I get to her room, her maid says she doesn't want company. Christian is on the stairwell leading to the third floor that is out of bounds to us. He catches me staring at him and stops walking. He tilts his head. I try my best to read something—*anything*—in his eyes, but they are a blank page.

I turn to leave but he speaks. "Wait a moment, Lady Ann."

"Yes, Prince Christian?"

"I get the feeling you had something more to say to me?"

"I wish that you would not be so hard on Lady Mary. She was only laughing at me; I was being clumsy. And she is crying in her room because you hurt her feelings."

"I should not have to do the job of a parent and scold her for misbehavior."

"You do realize she has a father and doesn't need a replacement? Mary came to the Palace looking for a husband, a partner, someone to confide in. And dare I say, *laugh with*. You may be a prince, but surely that gives you more reason to be kind to others," I spit back. "Especially when they are guests in your home."

"All I need in a wife is someone who can compose herself and bare me children."

"I wish you luck in finding that woman and may you never need to look to her to brighten your day, Prince Christian." And I leave, feeling his icy glare on the back of my head as I walk down the stairs.

At a loose end, I go to the library and smile at the books. They don't smile back, but they do bring me comfort. I want to read them all, but the sun's rays are reaching through the window and beckoning me to join them.

I grin and go upstairs to grab my camera, where I run into Mary coming out of her room. "Hey, Lady Mary, do you want to go for a walk with me outside? It could help you feel better."

"No thank you, Lady Ann. Prince Christian wants to have lunch with me. Isn't that great?"

"That's wonderful, Mary. Good luck and have fun." I give her a hug, to try to make her feel better about herself after this morning.

I spin around in the warm sunlight, greeting the cloudless blue sky as if it were an old friend. I slip my heels off with a groan and let my feet step free in the cool grass. With my camera at the ready, I alter the exposure and shutter speed, working on the ideal composition for pictures. The light is perfect, and I sit on a bench to take photos of the pond as the fish swim on the water's surface.

A reflection comes into focus and I jump back. "It's not nice to spy."

I get a chuckle in response as Prince Ryan comes closer. "I didn't want to intrude, Lady Ann. You looked as though you were in the zone, but I couldn't resist coming to see what you were up to."

"The zone? You sound familiar with artistic terminology."

"I consider myself a creative individual. I dabble in photography, painting, and sketching. Most of my time is spent on architecture though. What about you, Lady Ann?"

"Mostly, I farm. My dad and I have a ten-acre farm a few hours from here. I love to read, write, and take candid shots. What type of photos do you like to take, Ryan?" He is taken aback. Did I just call him by his first name? "I am so sorry, Prince Ryan." My arms are flailing as I try to cover my embarrassment. "You just seem so easy to talk to and you caught me off guard. I promise it won't happen again."

He laughs. "Ryan is fine, Ann. I am sure it is hard getting used to calling everyone by titles all the time."

"You're right. I tend to blurt out whatever is in my head, and when I'm talking to my hens, I don't have to think about protocol so much—though Henrietta does like a curtsy when I come for her eggs. But, yes, being here is a lot to get used to."

"Think nothing of it. It's a refreshing change to have a normal person treat me like a normal person."

I let out a nervous laugh, replaying my conversation with Prince Christian in my head. "Still no heels?"

"No, I am not brave enough."

"Oh, I doubt that."

"Listen, Ann, I came to warn you that Prince Christian is considering sending you home if you don't start acting more ladylike."

"Wow. That must be a new record for the history books. I don't think any Prince in the past has ever sent a candidate home during the first week before. But if he sends me home, then so be it. I want him to be happy, but I want to be happy too. If I change who I am, then I would be trading my happiness for someone else's, and that's not worth it." I don't know what else to say, or if I should thank him for his warning.

There's an awkward tension between us that wasn't there before. So, in an attempt to break it, I lift my camera and fire off some pictures of him. He laughs and closes the gap between us. He steals the camera from my hand and turns the tables, taking shots of me. I groan and try to grab it back. He holds it over my head. I jump for it. He falls backwards, trying to regain his balance.

I reach out to catch him, but it's too late, and he tumbles into the pond with a splash. I gasp and cover my mouth. He flounders around, trying to get out, and only succeeds in slipping again and I laugh so hard that I'm now crying. Ryan joins in my laughter as he climbs out of the pond. I offer him a helping hand, which he accepts.

"What is going on over here?"

I cringe and turn to Prince Christian. Our faces fall and we respond like naughty children caught misbehaving. "Your brother got too close to the edge of the pond and fell in."

"Oh, I bet he did. And why is it that every time I turn around, you are raising havoc?"

"Honestly, Christian, it's true, I tripped and Ann was helping me up. Please calm down. This is my fault, not hers."

Christian doesn't like the informality of Ryan using my first name. "We heard your noises from the sitting room. You are brainwashing my brother. Who the hell do you think you are? You will pack up and leave."

"You think you can judge me? I've done nothing wrong. I only expressed kindness and humor. But you can't have that, can you?" I poke my finger into his chest. "I pity the poor woman who has to marry such a coldhearted and judgmental man." We stare each other down, both on fire, and turn when we hear the crunching of grass.

"You three need to come inside with me." The Queen is flawlessly dressed in an elegant blue and white gown with gold shimmering heels. The beauty of her face is distorted as she glares at us. "This is disgraceful behavior." She walks back towards the Palace.

Christian grabs my arm, stopping me from leaving, and Ryan intervenes. "Let's go inside, Christian."

Christian releases me and stomps towards his mother. Ryan puts his hand on the small of my back to guide me inside.

"Ann, I am sorry. I should never have grabbed the camera from you. This is my fault." He enters the grand foyer with his clothes dripping wet. "I've made the situation worse and pushed him into sending you home."

"It's okay, Ryan. I was never going to belong here anyway."

The Queen is furious but speaks as calmly as she can. "Christian says Lady Ann is a bad influence on you, Ryan. And she's turned the Palace upside down with her inappropriate behavior."

"That's absurd, Mother. She's done no such thing."

"Lady Ann, what do you have to say about these accusations?"

"My Queen, I apologize for any trouble I've caused, and if this is how Prince Christian sees me, I am happy to pack my things and get out of his way."

"No, Lady Ann. Yes, you've heard me correctly — *no*."

Christian puffs out his chest. "With all due respect, Mother, you have no right. It is my choice, my future."

"Christian, my son. You have a lot to learn." She lets out an exasperated sigh. "How terrible would it look if you did not give the girls time to settle in before dismissing them?"

"I don't believe anything will change my opinion of Lady Ann." He clears his throat. "Fine, Mother, as you wish." With a nod towards the Queen, he exits. And I release a breath I didn't realize I was holding.

"Ryan, please go and change. You are dripping all over the carpet, dear." He nods and leaves us alone. Then the Queen turns to me. "Lady Ann, what is your honest opinion of Prince Christian?"

"Well, I have not known him long, my Queen, but from what I have witnessed so far, I think the bar he's set for finding a wife is unrealistic. He could miss out on something great because of it."

"I appreciate your honesty, Lady Ann. Do you think you can change his opinion of you?"

"I think it's doubtful I can change his opinion on anything."

"Why do you feel that way?"

"Because I'm just a farm girl. I wasn't raised for red velvet and fancy china. I feel that our worlds are very different, with very different views on how things should be."

The Queen smiles. "Can I let you in on a secret, Lady Ann?"

"Of course, you can, my Queen."

"I was just a farm girl when I was presented to King Mark. Do not think so little of yourself, Lady Ann. You can offer a unique perspective when it comes to what the country needs."

We discuss her various farming experiences, and I am dismissed several minutes later as she shuffles paperwork around.

Ryan is waiting outside my bedroom door, still soaking wet. "Ann, I am so sorry about your camera." Karen closes the door behind us as he stumbles inside. "I must have landed on it when I fell in the pond. But I'm going to find somebody to fix it. I promise."

A tear runs down my face as I think about my lost photos.

"Oh, Ann, please do not cry. I will make this right. You'll see." He grabs a nearby tissue box and I take it. Karen's disapproval is obvious, and he's sheepish when he turns to her. "Could you please grab Lady Ann something to eat? And maybe some water or tea?"

"Of course, Prince Ryan. I will be right back."

Ryan uses a tissue to wipe away my tears. "Do not change who you are for anyone, Ann. You are perfect just the way you are, and my brother's an idiot for not seeing it." Something between us shifts, but as quickly as it came, it's gone, and he takes his hand away. "How can I make this awful day up to you? What can I do to make you feel better?"

I'm still catching up with my emotions when Karen returns with a piece of dark-chocolate cake. While I eat, Ryan looks around my room and picks up the soft toy chicken.

"How about tomorrow I take you to the chicken house?"

"Chicken house?" I laugh and shake my head. "Sure. That sounds interesting."

"I will come for you first thing in the morning, and we can go." He squeezes my hand and walks out.

I laugh at his dripping, departing figure and turn to Karen. "Thank you, Karen. I appreciate your help. It's nice to have you around. Too bad I can't take you home with me when I return."

"You are welcome, my lady. If you continue to stroke my ego, I may consider making house calls. Is there anything else I can do for you?" She laughs as she gathers up my empty plate and cup.

I shake my head. "I had a rough start and I'm ready to call it quits for the day. Maybe I'll do some reading, have my meals in here, and take a bubble bath to try to soak out all of my negativity."

She sits at the edge of my bed. "I can bring some books up for you. And if you need someone to talk to, I am here for you too."

I place a hand on top of hers, to show my gratitude for her kindness. "That sounds perfect. Thank you."

When she comes back, I set the books on my table and we talk. I recap my awful day and she tells me about hers. Between the easy conversation, we share a meal of pea soup and fresh rolls. It's nice to have an ally in what feels like a hostile environment.

Opportunity

The following morning, I find Mary in the dining room sitting in the corner. I wave at her and she turns away to continue her conversation with another girl. The girl whispers in Mary's ear while her eyes watch me. They both throw their heads back and laugh before returning to their food. Blinking at the exchange in front of me, I feel my face get warm. I shake my head and stab at my eggs while the laughter dies down around me.

After breakfast, Ryan knocks on my door and Karen lets him in. "Ready to go see the chickens, Ann?"

"More ready than you will ever know," I grumble.

I feel my mood improve as the sun directs golden hues over the tall trees, and puffy clouds morph in front of my eyes. I squint and make out a cat leaping over an invisible obstacle. Our feet crunch on a gravel path. My heart races and my eyes glow as we approach an enclosed grey barn.

"Is this the chicken house, Ryan?"

He grins and flings the doors open. The combined smell of feathers, droppings, and death assaults my nose. I gag as I step inside. There are a hundred silver cages the size of shoeboxes. And in each one, there's either an egg-laying chicken or a much larger fowl raised for the table. The birds are distressed, many of them have bald patches from plucking their feathers in frustration, and some are bleeding from knocking against their cage. My heart sinks and my hands go to my mouth.

"These poor girls. What is this? How can you keep these poor animals like this? Can't you see they're suffering? It's inhumane. We need to help them."

"Ann, what's wrong? I don't understand. I thought you wanted to see the chickens."

"Yes, but not like this. They shouldn't be kept in tiny cages; they should be free to feel the sunshine and peck the ground. This is the most horrible thing I've ever seen."

"I will speak to the estate manager; however, I can't promise that anything will be done. This is the way it has been for a long time."

"These chickens are trapped, helpless, and waiting for their inevitable end. Would you like to live like this?" Tears well in my eyes as I shake my head. "Ryan, can you help me change this?"

"I can take you to my mom to discuss this with her, but my hands are tied."

I'm ready to take on the challenge. We enter the administration office. Twenty people are working in cubicles, at desks, and conference tables. Ryan knocks on the conference room door. Christian answers it and my stomach sinks. I aim to boost his mood by stroking his ego.

"This is amazing. I never realized how much work goes into running a country," I say to Christian's red face.

His eyes soften as he addresses his brother. "This is not part of show-and-tell time, Ryan. This area is off-limits for a reason. What is Lady Ann doing here?"

I look to Ryan, then to the Queen, who I notice is quietly watching with raised eyebrows. I must be careful with how I word this, because I don't want to ruffle any feathers, and tact isn't my strong point. I swallow and lift my chin. "Queen Elizabeth, this was my idea. I asked Prince Ryan to bring me. I know you, your family, and the Palace members all do your best to keep the country running as efficiently as possible. As you may recall, I was born and raised on a farm and I believe I can help with the chicken meat and egg production."

The Queen holds up a hand to still whatever Christian was going to say. "That is my department." She shuffles through some papers and puts on her reading glasses. "Our count has been steady. Have you heard something different?"

"With the greatest respect, I believe you can do better."

Christian is about to blow a gasket. "Are you kidding me? You spend a couple of days in our home and you think you can waltz in here and tell us how to run—not only our business—but an entire country? Your audacity is outrageous."

Ryan chimes in, "Christian, she just wants to help. Our chickens are living in appalling conditions. I had no idea how they were raised. And I can tell you it's *grim*."

"Ryan, stop defending her." The brothers face off like a pair of street fighters with balled fists. I rush between them trying to pull them apart.

The Queen stands and puts an end to the display before any punches are thrown. "Boys, take it outside, now," she says in a calm but authoritative tone.

I will Christian to be the bigger man. When he isn't, I put my hand on his arm. "Christian, I don't know why you dislike me so much, or why you're always yelling at your brother, but don't hurt him, please."

The Queen has had enough. "I said out. Now."

When the Princes have gone, I turn to their mother. "My Queen, I feel as though I am tearing your family apart. You should send me home."

"Lady Ann, you do not have any brothers, do you?"

"Um, no. I'm an only child but I don't see how that has anything to do with this situation, your highness."

"Well, my dear, boys do this. They fight over toys, sports, and pretty girls." She laughs and moves away from her chair as I blush. "Let me make you a deal, Lady Ann. You stay here and give us your best in this competition, and in return, you can hand me a report on how you can raise our production. And if it's cost-effective, I will give it proper consideration. How's that?"

"What if I'm no longer here because the Prince sends me home?"

She smiles. "Well, then I guess you have some work to do. And fast."

"Thank you. I appreciate this opportunity."

As I pass the library, I see the Princes bending over a table. Christian slips something into his pocket as his brother turns to me. "Ann. I have some great and some not-so-great news," Ryan says, then moves away from Christian. I look down at the table. There are hundreds of prints of my pictures from my broken camera laid out.

I smile from ear to ear. "Ryan, this is wonderful. Thank you."

"Actually, it has nothing to do with me, Lady Ann. Christian did it for you. I told him what happened, and he accessed the files, printed them, and made both a digital and a physical copy of each for you."

I can't believe that Christian "The Cold One" is actually blushing. "You? You did this for me? You have no idea how much this means to me. Thank you, Prince Christian." I gather them up to take to my room and probably overdo the *thank yous* in my excitement. The pictures of Ryan and me slide onto the floor and I pick them up. He has an excellent eye for photography.

Before I leave the library, I grab every chicken book I can find—there aren't many. However, I do have a heavy stack of reading material for the evening. When I get to the third stair, my foot turns inward, and I fall with a crash. Books land all over me and my ankle is burning. I try to stand but the pain is too much. People run to me from all directions and I'm instantly surrounded by some of the other women and servants.

"Are you okay, Lady Ann?" Mary asks as she offers me a slim, polished hand.

Remembering the incident from this morning, I glare at her fake kindness. "Yes, thank you."

Prince Christian comes around the corner. I groan internally. *Not again.* When I don't take Mary's palm, he offers me his. "Lady Ann, what happened to you?"

I accept his help but forget my ankle and cringe as I fall back down with a squeal. He catches me and wraps his arm around my waist.

"Lady Ann, are you hurt?" He frowns as my ankle swells.

"No, My Prince, I just thought I'd throw myself down the stairs for fun." I can't believe I said that. "Forgive me, Prince Christian. It's the pain. I fear it has made me irritable. I'm just a little sore and my pride is crushed. Thank you for the leg up." And I aim for my best—and what I hope is my most dazzling—smile.

"Ladies, I am going to escort Lady Ann to the hospital wing. Can one of you please take those... *chicken books* to her room. Thank you."

My eyes widen. "This is unnecessary, Prince Christian. I'm sure you are busy." But he insists on taking me to the hospital wing and helps me onto a bed.

"Get well soon, Lady Ann."

My ankle is blue and swollen. The doctor gives me some pain relief and takes x-rays. He tells me it's not broken, need to rest it. I'm given some crutches and he [on] a routine of ice, pain medication, and light duty [f]eels for a few days. He offers to have somebody [take me] back to my room, but I shake my head.

When I hobble out, Prince Christian is nowhere to be [fou]nd. I don't know why I expect him to be waiting for me. But I see him as being so stiff that his air of chivalry, and his need to be seen doing the right thing, would make it impossible for him not to be waiting. Clearly, I'm wrong.

My heart leaps as I see Ryan on the third floor. I wave to him, but he looks through me and disappears into another room. I set the crutches down and inch my way up the stairs, one at a time, using the banister to support me. The burning in my ankle intensifies. I hear a noise above and find Christian. "What are you doing, Lady Ann?"

I wipe the sweat from my forehead as I lean against the railing. I bite back my sarcastic remark. "Prince Christian, as much as it pains me to ask you, could you please help me up these evil stairs." I'm desperate, and even with my pain medication, I'm done pretending to be strong. I do need help but I refuse to beg. Either he helps me up or I will park myself here and stay forever.

In one swift movement, he lifts me up. The pain has made me sick and I feel dizzy. I wrap my arms around his neck and rest my head on his strong shoulder. I nestle into him and breathe in. He smells so good, like the woods after it

rains. I feel Christian tense. He opens my door and asks k
to pull back my covers.

"Lady Ann hurt her ankle and needs ice and rest. .
doctor gave her strong pain medication to help her sleep, s
she may be out of it for a bit. All of her meals are to be sent up
here for the next few days so that she can avoid the stairs."

"Yes, Prince Christian. I can get some water, ice, and a
light snack for her to help her sleep better. Would you like to
sit with her while I bring it? Or I can fetch another maid to
watch over her?"

"I can remain here until you return." Christian places
me on the bed. My brain is foggy, and the covers feel warm.
"Ann. You can let go now."

"So, it's just Ann, is it? No more Lady?"

"Lady Ann, please release me. You are making me feel
very uncomfortable."

"No. I like it here. And I like you not being mean and
fighting with me."

He laughs at my slurred words and tries to dislodge
my hand. I hold tight, thinking he's going to pry me off, but
he strokes my hair instead. "Why aren't you like everyone
else? Why are you so difficult?"

"Because I am Ann. I'm a farmer girl. And I am like no
one you will ever meet. I am special."

"Lady Ann, who do you think I am?"

"You are Prince Christian, the biggest pain in my
backside."

I am rewarded with one of his rare smiles. Then his eyes get smoky and he moves closer to my face. I hesitate, but my body has a mind of its own and closes the distance between us. Our lips meet and it's clumsy and awkward. I'm hot all over, and I feel sparks as he kisses me back and our bodies meld together as he deepens his embrace.

He pulls back and watches my eyes flutter open. "Lady Ann, smile for me, like no one else can." He says it huskily. My mind is hazy and sleepy, but I give him the most dazzling smile I can. Then he lays my head down, covers me up, puts a tender kiss on my forehead, and leaves as I drift off to sleep.

Dismissed

The pain medicine makes my dreams illogical. I vaguely recall chickens dancing on rainbows as I shuffle under my covers when the morning light reaches towards my face. When I wake up, my head is pounding, and my stomach is rolling. Thank goodness Karen is by my side with a bucket.

I cannot remember when I ate last, but whatever is in there comes out a lot faster than it went in. "Karen, please kill me. Kill. Me. Now." I lift my head out of the bucket and lie down as she applies ice to my ankle.

"Lady Ann, I am sorry, but I can't. At least not today." And she winks.

"Could you please just call me Ann? No *lady* business, at least when it's just us. I know Christian would crap his pants if he heard, but if you don't tell him, I won't... Speaking of Prince Christian, I had a dream about him where we kissed and he was so nice. He even called me Ann, just Ann. But that's not the real him. He wants perfection and I am not it. I would hate to be perfect." I shoo the thought away with a flick of my wrist.

Then she sits on the edge of my bed and grabs my hand. "That wasn't a dream. I walked in on him kissing you."

I feel myself go pale. "Oh, oh no. Karen, I need the bucket again."

She runs it over to me, and I dry heave. There's a knock on the door and it couldn't be a worse time. Karen places the bucket down to answer it. Ryan peeks his head around the door, and I hear laughter in the hallway and Christian's voice.

"Ryan, what the hell are you wearing?" Christian rings out.

I'm more curious than ever and forget about being sick. As Ryan enters, I hear tapping. He's wearing heels. I burst out laughing at the sight. He totters to the end of my bed, smirking. Christian comes in and shuts the door, but Ryan is the first to speak. "You don't look so good, Ann. Is there anything I can do?" Christian clears his throat and Ryan corrects himself. "*Lady Ann*, is there anything I can do for you?"

I tilt my head and cross my arms over my chest. "This doesn't make up for you dodging me last night, Prince Ryan. And I look bad? You are the one wearing death traps."

He clicks the shoes together. "I got Christian for you, didn't I? And regarding the heels, a deal is a deal. Pay up, lady."

"Fine. I am a woman of my word. The author of the quote was Dr. Seuss."

"Are you kidding me? Dr. Seuss?"

I laugh and the movement makes me queasy. I lean my head against the headboard. Ryan and Christian share a worried look, then Ryan asks Karen to get the doctor. "No, there's no need. I'm fine. Honestly."

Ryan hands me the silver heels, his older brother eyeing him intensely, then clears his throat and stammers,

"Lady Ann, I would like to tell you something of importance. I hope I've done nothing to give you the wrong impression, but I am engaged."

All of our encounters pass through my mind. Although I am inexperienced, I don't feel he gave me the wrong impression. We were friends. "Prince Ryan, I am happy for you. She is a lucky woman to have you as her fiancé. I hope I can meet her one day."

Ryan lets out a breath. "Of course, you will. Cherie is wonderful. I can't wait for you to meet her." The doctor arrives for my morning checkup, and Ryan squeezes my hand before leaving.

I am surprised that Christian stays by my bedside as the doctor shoves a thermometer in my mouth and a cuff on my arm. "Your maid filled me in, and I asked her to bring you some food. Your vitals and temperature look good." He removes the cuff and thermometer, pushes back the covers, and examines my ankle. "I think you had an allergic reaction to the pain medication. I'm putting you on an anti-inflammatory instead." The doctor closes his bag, nods at Christian, and shuts the door behind him.

I rub my arm where the cuff squeezed, while an uneasy tension blankets the room. Christian is back to his default setting of gloom and doom. All the humor and passion of last night has gone; it's as if it was a dream after all.

I blush and wring the sheet in my hands. "Christian, listen, about last night… I think I was out of line. I'm sorry. I would never have acted that way. The pain meds did a number on me."

He sits on the edge of my bed. "I am glad you are taking responsibility and admit that it was you who made the advances towards me, and that you were the one who was out of line. However, I need to take some blame too. I never should have let it get that far. But, Lady Ann, you drive me crazy. I am the future King of this country. I cannot lose control. I can't have a wife who is constantly battling me, falling all over the place, injuring herself, and inserting her opinions where she shouldn't. I need a Queen who will sit by my side with grace and elegance."

Karen reenters quietly and sets the tray down. I have been given weak tea, toast, and oatmeal. And it looks about as appealing as the man in front of me does. "Prince Christian, I am confused. You say I drive you crazy, and in the next breath, you say you don't want me. You're correct. I will never be that woman—the one sitting meekly next to your throne while obeying your every command. I would be somebody you can rely on. I would cope well in a crisis and work beside you with the country's interests in mind."

"Karen, please give me a moment with Lady Ann." Christian turns back to me. "Look at you. You are not Princess material. You don't have much of a figure and wouldn't carry the dresses well, you can't walk in heels, and you'd interfere all the time. You just would not do well as a Queen."

I force myself to listen.

"Lady Ann, once you heal, I expect you to pack your belongings and leave. You are no longer in the running to be my wife." He straightens his navy-blue suit, smooths out his hair, and nods with finality.

"I can't believe I agreed to stay, knowing you weren't going to try to make this work. I will be more than happy to leave."

Karen has been waiting at a discreet distance. When she sees Prince Christian stalking away with a look that could kill, she comes back to me.

"Karen, please help me pack and ready a car for me to return home."

"But what about the kiss?"

"I told you I must have been dreaming."

She packs my belongings and escorts me downstairs to the car. As we pass, the other girls pop their heads out of their rooms to see what the commotion is all about. Most of them are smug, smirking at me as I make my way down the hall.

Ryan comes running in our direction a few minutes later. He is out of breath by the time he reaches us. "Where are you going, Lady Ann?"

"Your brother said I don't fit the mold of a Queen."

Karen helps me into the waiting car and the driver loads my bags into the back. My ankle is on fire and I am sweating from the pain. I lean my head against the cool leather seats and let my eyes close.

Christian hammers on the car door. "What are you doing? I said to leave after you heal. This is senseless, and a perfect example as to what I said about your demeanor. Lady Ann. For goodness' sake, stop having to be the center of attention and get back inside immediately."

"No, thank you. I am leaving and going home, where I fit the mold of a farm girl. You can drop the formal title. I'm not in the running to be your wife."

"You are irrational. Come back inside on your own. Or I will carry you up those stairs."

"Don't you *dare* touch me."

When he slams the door, I know I've won. Ryan opens it again and hands me tissues. As I dab my eyes and blow my nose, he tells me, "Christian asked me to find someone to carry you upstairs. Ann, what do you want me to do? You can't travel like this."

"I don't belong here. Help me keep my dignity and let me go home to my dad."

"You need medical attention and rest. Look at you. How about a compromise? I'll carry you through a side entrance and no one will see. And I'll get you a temporary room downstairs. Just for a few days, until you can walk out of here on your own with your head held high. Then you can stick two fingers up at me, my brother, and all the other girls as you go. How's that? And what about our poor caged chickens? Are you going to abandon them and leave them to their fate? Lady Ann, I'm surprised at you."

"Fine, but you tell *his weenieness* that I am doing this for the chickens, and not because he told me to."

He laughs and repeats, "Weenieness?"

"Two days and that's it. I'll write the report and submit it, then I leave. Good enough?"

"Thank you, Ann. I am sorry he dismissed you. I think you would make a perfect Queen and an even better sister-in-law." He smiles and I can't help but return it. Ryan offers to carry me, but I bite my lip and shake my head. I use my crutches and take myself to my new room. It's smaller than the last one, with no windows. It has a tiny desk, a bathroom, two dressers, a pair of beds, and matching nightstands. Ryan says, "Karen offered to share her room with you, and she can help you until you leave."

I lower myself onto the bed, while Karen and a Palace guard bring my bags inside. Ryan gives my hand a squeeze and leaves. I smile at Karen and the guard. "Thank you both."

The tall man in uniform replies, "It's not a problem, Lady Ann. My name is Vinny. If you need any more help, let me know."

"Thank you, Vinny, but it's just Ann."

Vinny places my mountain of books on the desk.

"I owe both of you a lunch or something. Thank you so much for your help and hospitality."

Karen smiles. "Just get well and stay strong."

Vinny agrees. "I would love a lunch date." And he winks as Karen swats him playfully.

"Give her some recovery time."

I yawn and curl into a ball, wishing this was all a bad dream.

Bouncing Back

When I wake up, my stomach growls. Karen puts her book down. "Finally! I thought you were going to sleep forever. Do you have an appetite?"

"Yes, I'm starving."

As Karen gets breakfast, my thoughts drift to Christian. I could have pretended to be what he wanted and faked it to make it work. I mean, most of the girls surrounding him act like that. But that's not me. I have to be true to myself. I'm not letting one man make me question who I am.

Karen pulls me back to reality with the smell of biscuits and gravy and pancakes. I devour everything. "Thank you again, Karen. I feel better after eating. Could you pass me my books please?"

"I'm glad you are feeling better. You were looking pretty rough last night."

I grab my pencil and tap it against my lips. "Karen, what happens now? I mean with you. What will you do once I leave?"

"When you leave, I will just be a regular maid, doing this and that. Unless the Queen or Princess needs me, specifically."

"Do you like your job?"

"I like what I do. I don't have any complaints."

"I'm not sure what I want to do with my life. I mean, I thought I knew before I came here."

"You are a farmer. That is your passion. Do what you love, Ann. Or something related to what you love. That way you can be happy doing it. Otherwise, you will be miserable."

We spend a pleasant afternoon together, and I make a start on my report. I dedicate a few hours to reading and taking notes. My book pile dwindles as I absorb what I need from each. Pleased with what I've achieved, I put my books down and drift off to sleep.

When I'm feeling more rested, I try putting weight on my ankle. Pain shoots up my leg, but it's not as intense as it was yesterday. I stare at the ceiling and consider what Karen said about doing what I love.

The day passes into the next, and Karen is by my side with breakfast, coffee, and medicine. "You are too good to me."

"I'm just doing my job."

I shake my head between bites of scrambled egg. "It's more than that. You're obviously passionate about what you do, and you make me feel like I belong."

"Thank you, Ann. I appreciate that. How is your work going?"

"Great. I just have to type it up, hand it in, and cross my fingers. Is there a computer and printer I can use?"

"The servants have a break room. I can show you where it is when you're done with breakfast."

A few minutes later, we arrive at a busy room with computers, a television, tables, a fridge, a coffee maker, and a small library with red bean bag chairs. "This is amazing, Karen. I can see why you like your job and the benefits that go along with it." I log in to one of the computers and set about getting to work.

Karen makes coffee for us and sits on the couch, watching the news on the television. Palace employees trickle in and out of the room all day. I finish my report and stretch out my sore muscles. I rub my eyes and blink away the burned image of the screen from the backs of my eyelids. Karen retrieves my documents from the printer as Vinny comes in. He grabs the papers from Karen's hands before she can stop him.

"Well, well, well. What is this?" His eyes scan the pages. He's in jeans and a white t-shirt and his hair is ruffled. I hold my breath, waiting for his opinion even though he didn't ask my permission to read my work, as he turns to Karen. "Wow, Karen, beauty and brains. This is great. I didn't know you could write like this."

She snatches the papers and hands them to me. "I didn't write it, Ann did."

"That report is very thorough." He winks and goes to the coffee maker.

I read through the documents twice, editing where I can, and ask Karen to skim them too, just to see if any glaring errors leap out at her. Even with her help, though, I don't feel confident in my writing. I would be humiliated if the Queen were to think it's juvenile during her review. "Vinny, could you please take another look?"

He gets up and sits next to me in an empty chair. "Are you sure? I don't know if I have both brains *and* muscle."

"I'm sure there's more to you than meets the eye." I chuckle.

"It's great, Ann. I fixed a few minor details."

I get Karen's vote of approval. "Thank you, Karen. I appreciate your help."

"I'm going to grab our laundry and make some food. See you in a bit, Ann."

I wait for Vinny to finish. He's smarter than he lets on and helps me reorganize some paragraphs to make the overall composition better. It reads well, as I type in the changes, reread it, and reprint it. He looks it over once more and hands it back to me.

"Thank you, Vinny. It reads a lot better and flows well."

"I'm always willing to help a lady in need."

Karen rushes in with a hand to her chest. She's breathless. "Ann, I forgot the doctor was coming to check on your ankle. He's looking for you."

"These crutches aren't very fast, but I'll do my best to get there as quickly as possible." I push to my feet and hobble towards her room. Vinny scoops me up in his arms, and I squeal as my crutches crash to the floor.

"Vinny, this is completely unnecessary. Put me down."

"Karen, grab her stuff and meet us there," he shouts over his shoulder as he carries me. "It will be faster. Don't worry. I won't drop you."

"My hero." I laugh.

"You're right: all soldiers are heroes, Ann." Vinny sets me down while nodding towards the older man in the white coat. "Good luck with this one, doc." Then he winks at me and speaks to the figure lurking in the dark corner of the room. "Good afternoon, Prince Christian."

The doctor checks the progress of my healing ankle. "The swelling has gone down, Lady Ann. You should be ready for regular duty in no time."

"I'm eager to leave as soon as possible. When can I travel home?"

The doctor turns to Christian. "I see no reason she can't travel now. Lady Ann, just take it slow and try not to reinjure it." He packs his stuff into his medical bag and nods towards his employer. "Is there anything else I can do for you, Prince Christian?"

Christian thanks the man for his time. Karen comes in after the doctor has gone and sees my unwanted guest lurking in the background. "Oh, Prince Christian, can I get you something?"

Before he can respond, I chime in, "Karen, can you please hand me my crutches?" She passes them to me and I get up to leave. "Are you ready for lunch?" I ask her.

"Lady Ann..." Christian steps forward to address me.

And I'm frozen in place as those two simple words roll off his tongue. Karen squeezes my hand before she walks off. "How about we have lunch together instead?" he adds.

"I would rather not."

"I thought you were making plans to eat with your maid a second ago?"

"No, I was going to have lunch with my friend."

"And the guard? Were you planning on meeting him too?"

I try not to notice the loose strand of blonde hair falling over his forehead. He rubs his temples and pushes the stray end back in place.

"I came all this way to check on you, Lady Ann. Only to find you in another man's arms."

My jaw drops. "Correct me if I'm wrong, Prince Christian," I spit. "But you sent me home because you were absolutely sure I wasn't what you were looking for. Does it surprise you that another man may want what you don't?"

He frowns down at me. "Just because I don't want you as my wife doesn't mean I don't want you at all."

"Prince Christian, that makes no sense to me."

"Ann," Karen calls as she runs towards me in the hallway.

"Karen, slow down. What happened?" I ask as the Prince comes up behind me.

"Your dad, he's in the hospital," she pants between breaths.

I absorb her words, my knees go weak, and I feel myself falling in slow motion. Christian catches me. "Ann. Are you okay?" His concerned voice seems far off as images of my past haunt me. I remember being at my mother's death bed. Saying goodbye to her... I can still feel her cold hand in mine. I shiver and shake my head.

Karen moves closer. "Ann, they said he is in stable condition. Try not to worry too much. I'm sure he'll be okay."

"I need to leave and go to him."

Karen helps me pack up my things and it isn't long before there's a car waiting for us. Christian is standing and talking to the driver as we pile everything into the trunk, and a new wave of tears suddenly blurs my vision. I hug Karen tight before turning back towards the Prince.

I pull him into my arms and hold him there a moment, willing his strength and composure to seep into my weary soul. He tickles my neck as he whispers to me, "Don't give up on us, Ann. I will figure something out. Can we be friends, for now?"

"After everything that's happened here, I don't know if I can. If we can." The car pulls off down the drive and I watch his somber expression as he watches the taillights fade away. The rain patters against the window, obscuring my view of the town and reflecting my mood. What a mess my life is. It's filled with pain, sprinkled only by short intermissions of joy.

Home

I decide to drop my bags off at home before checking in on my dad. As much as I want to see him, I want to avoid the inevitable attention I would receive at the hospital when I pull up in a Palace vehicle. The driver grabs my bags and helps me in the door. I try turning on the lights, but they aren't working.

"It must be a tripped breaker. I can fix it easily. Thank you for all your help. I hope you have a safe drive back." I wave as I watch the driver pull away. Then growl and toss the crutches aside. I'm done trying to maneuver around the house in the dark with those monstrosities.

I limp towards the garage, using my hands to guide me, and chew my lip as I tap the metal box. All the breakers are in their correct positions.

The phone rings, pulling me out of my stupor. "Hello?"

"Ann, did you make it home safely?" It's the all-confusing Christian.

"I didn't expect you to call." I rub my face as I sit on the bar stool.

"Why not? I'm making sure that my friend made it home safely. That's acceptable, isn't it?"

"I'm not sure about being your friend, but I am home."

There's a long silence on the line, and then he says, "Ann, you sound tense. Are you all right?"

"You mean other than being worried sick about my dad in the hospital?" When he doesn't respond, I continue my tirade. "Now, on top of everything else, my power is out and I'm not sure why." I rub my tense neck. "This isn't your fault. I'm sorry. Thank you for checking up on me. But I need to go."

"Well, let me help. I will call the power company while you get ready to see your father. How about we meet back on the phone in fifteen minutes?"

"You'd do that for me? That is very considerate of you. Thanks."

With fifteen minutes to kill, I do what I always do in times of crisis, or whenever I'm feeling low: I go outside to talk to my chickens. I call out to them and they run over—and you don't need to be Doctor Doolittle to know that they're complaining bitterly about their lack of food and water.

I say a quick hello and try to fill their water bottles, but nothing comes out of the hose. "What's going on here?" I ask Pecker as she waits by my side. Suddenly, the security and porch lights turn on, and water shoots out of the hose, scaring Pecker and soaking me. She pecks at the newly formed puddle on the ground. All thirty hens fight to get water as I collect the neglected eggs in the henhouse. I kneel to stroke the girls' colorful feathers and they look at my empty hands.

Hearing the phone ring again, I run inside, tripping over Pecker as I go. "Hello?"

"Why are you out of breath? Is everything okay?" Christian asks.

"Yeah, no, I don't know. I am totally confused. The power and water weren't working and then they came on a few minutes ago. The ladies have no food or water. I'm not sure how long they have been in that state, and this isn't like my dad."

"That does sound odd. How many people live in your house?"

"It's just me and my dad."

"So what ladies have you so concerned?"

"Oh, I'm sorry. I know it's silly, but I call the chickens *ladies*." I sigh. "Thank you for your help, Christian. Did the power company say what was wrong?"

"This is a bit awkward to disclose; however, your dad may have forgotten to pay the utility bills. But don't worry I paid them, and we have everything back on for you."

"I'll figure out what happened and pay you back."

He laughs. "Do not worry about it. I can afford it."

"No, Christian. I'm serious."

"Fine, but I do not want your money. How about dinner or lunch?"

I imagine him smiling on the other end of the phone, his confidence evident in both is tone and expression. "Fine, if I'm ever in the neighborhood, I'll take you to dinner."

"No. I want a nice meal, just you and me," he replies softly.

"Okay, if I'm in the neighborhood, I'll have a *nice* meal with you. How are you?"

"I am doing well. Thank you for asking. I'm going to allow some of the ladies to go home tonight, and I am working on my speech," he says in his best business voice.

I grin. "Oh, you mean your chickens?"

"No, Ann, I do not mean chickens."

I clear my throat. "So how is your family?"

"Mom and Dad are fine. Ryan went to visit his fiancée because they got into a fight."

"Oh, that's not good. Nothing serious I hope?"

"Do not worry yourself. I am sure Ryan and Cherie can work it out."

"Well, it's getting late. I should get to the hospital before visiting hours are over."

"I can call you later... if it's not too late?"

"Okay, I'll speak to you later. And, Christian? Thank you again for fixing this mess for me. I don't think I would've been able to figure it out as fast as you did."

"Of course. I miss you, Ann."

"Christian, please don't... It's not fair."

"I'll talk to you soon."

When I arrive, I check in at the front desk of the hospital with sweaty palms and a racing heart, remembering the outcome of the last time I was here. Nothing has changed. The short-haired nurse smiles and directs me to my dad's room. I knock on the door. Opening it, I blink when I see my dad sitting in a hospital gown, laughing with our neighbor Suzie.

"Ann? Is that really you?" He raises his arms for a hug.

"I thought I was going to lose you. What happened?"

"I wasn't feeling well. Then I started having chest pains and Suzie brought me to the emergency room. It's nothing major. They are just keeping me overnight for observation."

"Why was the power off at the house? And the chickens were hungry and left without food."

My dad blushes, and Suzie clears her throat. "Jack, honey, I'll be right back. I am going to check my voicemail real fast." She smiles at me. "It is nice to have you home, Ann."

I fall into a chair at his bedside. "What did Suzie just call you?"

"I'm sorry I forgot to pay the bills. I mean, you always did that for me. And, to be honest, I haven't been home a lot. I've been over Suzie's. I've been lonely for a long time, my darling. You know nobody will ever replace your mom, but we are dating."

I jump up from my chair as my face quickly pales, then reddens. "What? So you just abandoned the chickens. And our home. If I hadn't returned, would you have just carried on with your girlfriend and left the hens neglected until they starved?"

He looks tired and more his age than I've seen in a long time. "Ann, that's not what happened. Suzie is a wonderful woman, but no one will ever replace your mother or our chickens. Wait a minute… Why *are* you home, sweetheart?"

.   I stare at my feet. "Sorry, Dad, but I let you down. I'm not princessy enough to be a Princess and Prince Christian sent me home."

Suzie reenters the room, and my dad immediately beams at her. She grabs his other hand and I tug mine away.

"I'm going to take a walk and get some air."

There's a television in the corner of the waiting room. The news is on and showing pictures of Prince Christian and each of the girls in the competition—including me.

"Tonight, we are pleased to announce the shortlist of the Prince's favorite girls. Let's give them a hand and wish the Prince good luck with this life-altering decision. In other news, our inside sources say that one of the participants has a secret crush on Prince Ryan and that is why she was sent home. Naughty, naughty. Now the younger Royal is with his fiancée, trying to patch things up."

I realize I opened myself up to public scrutiny when my dad entered me into the competition, but I am furious that my private life is laid bare—and on national television too.

I call Christian, and an unknown male voice answers, "Prince Christian's room. How may I assist you?"

"Is the Prince available, please?"

"May I ask who is calling?"

"Ann."

I hear mumbling in the background and Christian comes on. "Ann, how is your father doing?"

"He is sleeping with our neighbor, apparently. I leave for five minutes and she slides right in. Oh, and he blames me for not remembering to pay the bills. I mean, who does that? He is a grown man."

Ever the diplomat, Christian's best answer is, "Oh, well, that is interesting. Is your father feeling better?"

"Oh, sorry. Yes, they are keeping him overnight for observation. So I've just been watching the news. Congratulations, by the way. It looks like you were able to narrow down your search."

"Yes, I guess congratulations are in order. I am sorry you had a rough night, Ann, but I am glad your father is feeling well."

"Thank you for the ear, but I should get back in there before visiting hours are over and the dad-stealer gets engaged to him or something while I'm away grabbing a coffee."

He chuckles and clears his throat. "I understand. But, Ann, may I make a suggestion?"

"Yes, Christian?"

"Try to go easy on your neighbor. You can sometimes come off as, well, a little... abrupt."

"Really? Well, that makes two of us."

"What do you mean by that?"

"Oh, come on, you know exactly what I mean. If we're talking about inflexibility, you take the cake with your set-in-stone standards for an impossibly perfect wife."

There's a long silence on the other end of the phone. "Have a good night." And he hangs up.

I try to appear calm, when I return to Dad and Suzie, and take a moment to watch them interact. They pause mid-conversation. "Ann, sweetie, there is no need for you to stay here with me. I promise I'm fine, and I'll be home tomorrow after the doctor makes his rounds."

I get up and hug him. "I see how it is, Dad. You're kicking me out after everything I did for you." I elbow him. "I'm glad you are feeling better, though." I kiss his forehead. "I'll see you in the morning. Try to get some rest."

Before heading back to the farm, I buy some chicken food at the store. And when I arrive home, I feed and put the chickens away in their pen. After finding Pecker in her bush, I give her a kiss and hug and shut her away with the rest of the girls.

"Good night, ladies. Sleep well. I will see you in the morning."

That night, I stare at the ceiling and replay the hospital visit. I turn to my side and feel a warm tear roll down my cheek. My dad sent me away so easily. Is he disappointed in me because I was dismissed by the Palace?

I toss and turn until I fall into a fitful sleep, dreaming that it's raining white feathers all around me. I'm running towards a dark shadow, but I don't know what it is. I can feel that it's important. But no matter how close I get, I end up farther away. Soon, the white feathers are flooding the room as they suffocate me.

Committee

I wake before the rooster crows. I'm exhausted but start my old routine—and a big cleanup of the house and farm. Cleaning clearly hasn't been on top of my dad's agenda while I've been away. After a cup of coffee, I feed, water, and tidy the chicken yard. Then I come inside to make some fresh eggs for breakfast. As I finish eating and wash my dishes, Dad and Suzie walk through the front door, laughing and holding hands.

"There's my baby girl." He comes over and hugs me.

"I'm so glad to see that you're feeling better, Dad."

"I'm going to shower and wash this hospital smell off me. Can you keep Suzie entertained while I'm gone, please?"

My neighbor sits on the couch and pats a spot next to her. "What is going on, Ann? What happened at the Palace? Did you not like it? Or was it *him* you didn't like?"

I ignore her invitation for comradery and cross my arms over my chest. "Maybe *he* didn't like *me*."

"No, I don't think that's it. How could anybody not like you?"

My lip trembles. Her words sting. "Well, you are wrong." I slump down beside her on the couch, battling the tears threatening to spill free. "Physically we have a connection but it's, well, I don't know. Every time we are together, it's like he's two different people. One wants to be with me and will let me in, while the other is closed-off and closed-minded. He sent me home, saying I didn't fit the mold for a Queen."

A few tears fall. I realize I'm being petulant, and that it's half to do with Prince Christian and half to do with how she muscled in on Dad the minute my back was turned. He's my dad—and he's all I have in this upside-down world.

Suzie grabs my hand. "Oh, Ann, I'm sorry. You are a strong, independent woman. And sometimes that scares men. They feel less needed and respected. Maybe what you two need is a compromise? For you to rely on him a little and he on you? And that *fit the mold* crap? Well, that is just ridiculous, and he will see it eventually. Physical characteristics come and go; they change with each season. You need to love someone and want to be with them for what is on the inside."

"But it's too late. I've already lost him."

"Oh, Ann, it's not over until you hear those wedding bells. Don't give up if that's what you want, my dear. I am always here for you, if you ever need me. And I promise I won't let your dad slack on his responsibilities again." She pats my leg and moves to the kitchen. I hear our coffee machine start up. Then the phone rings and she answers it. "Ann, it's for you."

"Hello?"

"Hey, it's Karen."

"Karen? Oh, man, I've missed you. What's going on at the Palace? Did you get stuck on toilet duty yet? Or does Lady Mary have you massaging her feet?"

"Very funny. Actually, I turned in your report. The Queen asked me to call you and see if you would come back and review it with the committee tomorrow."

"My dad was only just discharged from the hospital this morning, and I can't leave again so quickly."

Suzie pokes my side and mouths, "It's not over."

Karen continues. "Ann, this is a great opportunity for you. Think about it. If you're offered a job, it'll mean a considerable salary. Not to mention all the experience and contacts you'll make. Plus, there's the biggest bonus of living with your best friend again."

I laugh and my body relaxes. "Karen, I don't know." I bite my fingernail as images of Christian flood my mind.

My dad comes into the kitchen and wraps an arm around Suzie. "What doesn't Ann know?" She whispers in his ear, and he adds, "Oh, Ann, tell her yes. I will drive you to the Palace myself if I have to."

"Dad," I groan and hear Karen laugh.

"Actually, Queen Elizabeth offered to send a car to pick you up. It can leave as soon as you say yes. Come on, Ann. Do It. Don't make me beg."

"Oh, so this hasn't been you begging?"

"Not yet."

"Fine, but I expect to see you in the car when it arrives." I can hear her jumping up and down. "Awesome, I'm on my way. See you soon."

I turn to pack and blink at Suzie and my dad as they watch me.

"So, Prince Christian asked for you to come back?"

"Actually, Dad, the Queen has asked me to speak to a committee. She hopes to raise their egg and meat production, and because I had a few ideas for their husbandry and produce, she's asked me to consult on it."

"That is wonderful, Ann. I'm so proud of you. The Queen wants my girl to raise her chickens. I'll make everyone sandwiches to celebrate."

"Don't get too excited, Dad. I'm only helping them rebuild their chicken coop and teaching them how to free range—that's all." Although I must admit my heart swells with his words. When I'm ready to leave and waiting for Karen, I decide to eat with Dad and Suzie. "Are you sure you'll be all right without me?"

"I will be more than all right, sweetheart. I have a great nurse looking after me. And I know you'll hurry back if I need you." Dad answers the door and Karen flies in. I introduce everyone and offer her the grand tour. I show her the chicken yard, the house, and the property. She loves our fruit trees and large garden.

"This is beautiful, Ann. No wonder you love it so much."

I take in a long breath as we look out at the yard. "It is definitely hard to leave this place again." We return to the main house and give everyone hugs.

"Well, your chariot awaits, my Lady." Karen grins and offers a bow.

I force a smile. After being sent home, I'm not a Lady in the Palace. I'm just another servant helping the Queen. And it is a good reminder of how much things will change when I go back. "Thank you for coming to get me, Karen."

She locks arms with me and we place my bags in the car. I hug Dad—and even Suzie—and remind them to pay the bills and keep an eye on the chickens until I return.

Throughout the drive, Karen talks to me about her life and how she and Vinny have been hanging out a bit. I get the feeling they may be building more than a friendship, because of the way her eyes glitter as she talks about him and the things they do together. I love listening to her and watching her expressions, and I wonder if she knows she is making them. I know she's falling for her friend, even if she doesn't.

After a while, she asks me to update her on what's been going on with me, so I tell her about my dad and Suzie, the house and chickens, and Christian and our last phone conversation.

"Hey, I am sure everything will work out." She pats my hand gently and I pray that she's right.

I'm staying with Karen again and it's late when we arrive at the Palace. She grabs us some food and we eat in the room, then climb under the covers.

In the morning, I lie awake in my bed. I bet the roosters aren't even crowing yet. I slip out of bed quietly. Then there's a knock on the door. It's one of the Queen's maids. "Good morning, Lady Ann."

"Actually, it's just Ann. I'm not in the competition anymore."

"I'm sorry. Just Ann it is then. Queen Elizabeth has asked me to collect you and bring you to her quarters."

"Her room? But why? Isn't that off-limits?"

"Ann, I am only doing what I'm told to do."

Karen is stirring and she waves her arm at me. "Go already. It is my day off and I need my beauty rest."

So I follow the woman out, and we take a new route through the servant's quarters. It's busy and people brush past us with trays and towels. The Palace is quiet except for its designated worker bees. The maid knocks on a set of heavy wooden doors.

"Come in," the Queen answers.

My face turns red as I realize I'm still in my old nightgown. But the tension leaves me when I enter and note that the Queen is in a soft-pink, silk nightgown that hugs her frame.

"Ann, it is wonderful to see you again. You know, my dear, it has been quieter without you." She winks at me. "I hope your father is home and doing well?"

"Yes, my Queen. He is feeling better and at home."

"That is good to hear, Ann. Now we may speak about other business. I know that since you left you have been going by Ann, but that needs to change. If you want to improve the welfare of our livestock, then you need the committee to take you seriously. And for that, you need a suitable title, my girl. Also, I need you to look your best today. Most of the committee members are male, and the only way to get their attention is to, well, you know, *get there attention*. You must look your best and appear confident. Now, what do we have here?" She moves through her closet and pulls out all kinds of styles of dresses, shoes, and jewelry. She motions for a maid to grab them. Then she stops fidgeting with her wardrobe and looks at me. "If you want to leave, I understand. This is your chance to turn me down and head home. However, if you stay, I promise it will be in your best interest and you will make some positive changes."

I need coffee. It's too early to take all this in. "I have never given up on anything before, but I have to be honest. I am not looking forward to going back to wearing dresses and being called a Lady again."

She laughs and sits next to me. "I find your honesty refreshing. I understand. I never wanted any of this either." She motions to her room. "I just fell in love with a man and everything else fell into place." She passes me several options. "Ann, here are some things for you to try on. You can go into the bathroom and change whenever you are ready."

I close my eyes as her maid works on me. The woman pokes, pulls, and powders. And when she's done, she says, "Okay, open your eyes."

I peek with one eye, then the other. My hair is pulled up, my face is painted with lipstick and gloss, my dress is light blue with little gold flecks, and my shoes (thank goodness) are flats. "Thank you."

"My pleasure, Lady Ann. How about we show the Queen?"

The Queen is in a beautiful lavender dress with light-pink accents. She beams at me. "Absolutely beautiful. Great job, Adrie."

"Thank you. I hope I don't make a fool of myself. I'm great with animals and books, but not so much with people."

"I am confident that you can win them over. Have more faith in your abilities. Are you ready, my dear?"

I swallow, grateful for my empty stomach. She opens the door and ushers me into a huge ballroom with tables and a podium. Not many people are in attendance at the moment, but I expect that to change.

The Queen guides me to a table on the stage. "Lady Ann, we will sit up here. They will serve breakfast to everyone. After that, I will make a short speech and introduce you. Then you can present your findings to the room, and we'll open the floor for questions and hold a vote."

The blood drains from my face as my eyes dart from the podium to the Queen.

"Do not worry, you will do great."

King Mark enters in a blue suit and leans down to kiss his wife's cheek, then he turns to me. "Good day, Lady Ann.

I am pleased you could return to the Palace for this opportunity. My wife has been very enthusiastic about making these positive changes."

I am distracted by the wonderful smell of fresh coffee. The butlers serve us, and the room fills to the brim. The Queen was right about the ratio of men to women; there are a lot more of the former. I squirm on the inside but try to look calm and confident.

Christian enters the room, and I feel my world shift. My lips pull back in something that might be a smile. He fixes his expression into a more neutral one as he greets the people closest to him.

I lean towards the Queen as she sips her coffee and whisper, "Did the Prince know I was coming for this meeting?"

"I guess it must have slipped my mind."

Christian approaches and kisses her cheek. He nods at me in greeting. The King turns to him and they engage in quiet conversation.

The waiters serve our food and it smells delicious; however, in this dress and with my speech looming, I only poke at it. We eat with little small talk, and I can feel Christian's eyes on me, but I sit tall and behave appropriately.

The Queen turns to me. "Here we go, Lady Ann." Then faces the crowd. "Good morning, ladies and gentlemen. Thank you for coming to our annual committee meeting. I hope everyone enjoyed their breakfast." We applaud politely and she talks about how well the committee has been running and how the newly implemented improvements are coming along. She expresses how excited she is to introduce a new idea for discussion. "Here to guide us today is my new friend: Lady Ann." The crowd claps as we switch places, and she whispers, "You can do this."

I am standing in front of what feels like a hundred people—though I haven't counted. I swallow and will the sweat not to ruin my makeup before delving into my research. I talk about chickens, egg and meat production, sanitation, and share my collected data and predictions. As I speak on some of my favorite topics, I realize how silly I was for being nervous. Soon, I conclude my findings and open the floor to questions. The first few are about the startup costs and potential timeframes.

Then somewhere in the crowd a male voice asks, "Are you single?"

I'm thrown off as everyone laughs, and I feel my face get warm. I move on quickly. "Any other questions?" And we are back on track. "Thank you for your time and consideration, ladies and gentlemen. I hope that I have given you enough information to see the viability of my proposal this morning." I step off to applause and the King takes my place at the podium.

"Thank you, Lady Ann. If there are no more questions, let us take a vote. All those in favor of the new changes raise your hand." It's unanimous. "All those opposed?" Nobody raises a hand. "Then it is decided. We will move forward with the modifications. Thank you for joining us and enjoy the rest of your day."

"You did wonderfully, Lady Ann. Welcome to the team." The Queen helps me down the stairs, and I'm introduced to so many people it's a blur of faces and names. Until most of them file out and Christian comes over with his dad.

"Prince Christian. King Mark."

The King gives his son a look before offering his goodbyes to the remaining attendees. Christian touches my elbow to get my attention. "Lady Ann, that was very well executed. I'm impressed with your speech delivery. I look forward to learning more about your countless other abilities."

"As we all are," a new male voice interjects from behind Christian. I turn to a man of medium height, with wavy brown hair and dark eyes. He runs a hand down his light-grey suit and adds, "Who would have guessed such a beauty could be intelligent too?"

I look from Christian to the newcomer, hoping to be introduced. When that doesn't happen, I extend a hand myself. "I'm sorry but I don't believe we've met. I'm Lady Ann, and you are?"

"It's nice to meet you, Lady Ann. My name is Kevin. I work here in the finance department. I'm sure we will be seeing more of each other."

I pull my hand back. "It's very nice to meet you too, Kevin."

He turns to Christian. "I can't imagine why you let her go. But I'm not complaining."

The Queen walks past me and suggests, "Let's get changed and we can start our work."

Before we reach her room, Christian asks, "Lady Ann, wait a minute, please."

I hesitate and look at the Queen, then at Christian's door. She pauses to reply, "Christian, dear, we have a lot to do in the office. Is there any way this can wait?"

"This will only take a few minutes, Mom."

"You have five, Christian. I will be with Adrie when you are done."

My eyes grow wide as the Queen closes her door and leaves me with her son. "Yes, Prince Christian?"

"I will not bite, Lady Ann. Come inside my room please."

I step over the threshold and into the massive bedroom. On the walls are pictures of faraway places and images of Christian with important people. I run my hand over an image of him as a little boy at the beach. You can see how happy he is as he holds a shell up to whoever's behind the camera. He is more carefree now than he appeared earlier, but he has lost the innocence he had as a boy as well as the spark of life that's so apparent in the photo.

"Could you please excuse us for a moment, Jerry?" he asks his butler. Christian steps closer to me and puts his warm hands on my face. And I stop breathing.

I swallow hard. "I thought you wanted to talk?"

"Hush, I only have five minutes." He dazzles me with one of his rare, relaxed smiles. He touches his lips to mine and my world spins. I forget about being sent home, and all I want are his kisses and his passion. I can feel how much he wants to be with me. There is magic in his kiss. It's perfect. But as the kiss deepens, my conscience takes over. And all his harsh words are on repeat in my mind.

I pull away from him. "Christian, I thought you said we could be friends. Please, we can't do this."

"Of course, we can. Your lips, my lips—together—it's simple really."

"You told me to leave. I'm here strictly on business and that's it. And if you can't handle being friends, I can change it to only being coworkers." My back hits his dresser as I put distance between our hot bodies. And my eyes drop to a picture in a beautiful silver frame. It's the picture Ryan took. Of me. "Christian, what is this? Where did you get this?" I gesture to the photo.

"I wanted to remember you."

"You tell me one thing and show me another—I don't know where I stand with you. You need to control yourself and stop sending me mixed messages. It's not fair." I lower my gaze and brush past him.

The Queen doesn't ask about my conversation with Christian when I return to her. "Ann, we need to discuss some things before you leave."

I cringe. "Of course, my Queen. What would you like to discuss?"

"Which bedroom are you staying in?"

"I'm staying with Karen, in the servants' quarters. She was my maid and we've become good friends."

She purses her lips. "Well, for the time being, I would like you closer to the office. I think it would be best if we assign Karen to you again and move you into a guest room. Here, on the third floor."

"My Queen, I have no problem moving if you want that, but I am worried about Christian. I think he is having a hard time focusing on the remaining girls, and I don't want him to think that I am still one of his participants." My face is burning.

"I have noticed how Christian is around you, and I am embarrassed to admit I was hoping he would ask you to marry him. You offer him a fresh perspective."

"What? But it's too late. He sent me home."

"The rules say he only has to choose from the selected girls, and you were one of those selected."

I try to process what she's telling me. "Does Prince Christian know this?"

She nods but frowns. "Ann, I'm his mother, so I can say this to you. My son is naive. He thinks he has to behave a certain way as the future King. And, naturally, he feels that his chosen Queen should behave in a similar manner. I know what I would like him to do; however, I can't make his choices for him. But never mind all these *what ifs*. If it would make you more comfortable, I will station a guard outside your room and have him escort you around. But it won't stop the natural forces at work. Whatever will be, will be. Now, we have work to do and I want to finish it before Christmas."

My head is spinning with the Queen's words as I follow Adrie to my new room. I thought this competition nightmare was over. And yet I have an eerie feeling that it has only just begun.

I glance around my new room. It's another extravagant suite. It's beautifully decorated, clean, and airy, with lots of natural light. I thank Adrie and fall onto the bed as she closes the door.

Will Christian decide that he made a mistake in sending me home? Will he set aside everything he thinks he knows and choose me? I put my finger to my mouth, remembering the kiss we shared.

Karen comes in with a huge grin. She twirls around the open space. "Oh, Ann. This is beautiful. I am so glad to move up here with you." She falls onto the bed next to me. "Thanks for bringing me back. I hated kitchen duty."

"Hey, stop complaining. It's better than toilet duty. And if you ever call me *Lady Ann* when we're alone, I'll ask the Queen to put you on it." I grab a pillow and toss it at her face.

She reaches for her own and gives it to me as good as she gets it. Feathers are flying when there's a knock on the door and Vinny pops his head in. "Hello. I heard a couple of special ladies have moved up here. And, seeing as I'm going to be taking on more duties on this floor, I'm at your service should you need anything."

We look at him, then at each other, and without having to say anything, we throw our pillows at him. He laughs and tosses them back.

"I'm so glad to have friends around me. I missed you both," I say. "Now get out, Vinny. I need to change. I have some chickens to save."

Karen opens the fully-stocked closet. "Okay, Mistress Ann, it's time to play dress up." We sift through all the options and I change into a light-blue sundress. Karen polishes my face and pulls my hair up.

I look in the mirror and have never felt so blessed. I've never had so many beautiful things, but they pale in comparison to having two new best friends. And I realize that while my life on the farm was idyllic, it has been lonely since my mother died. The nature of farming, as well as my family home's distance from town, means I've been severely lacking in making friends my own age.

"Thank you, Karen."

She winks at my reflection. "Now go knock 'em dead."

Duties

I stop short in front of the office doors. Vinny plows into my back as he follows. "Sorry, Ann. Is something wrong?" he asks as he glances from side to side with a hand near his holster.

I release the insecurities floating around me and hold myself tall. I walk into the Queen's office and I am relieved that Christian isn't waiting for me. We work on designs for the new coop, a fenced enclosure, feeders, and water troughs. By lunchtime, we are pleased with what we've achieved and our stomachs growl.

I go to my room in search of Karen. With a hand on my doorknob, I pause, hearing noises coming from the dark hallway in front of me. Vinny puts his arm out. "I wouldn't go that way if I were you."

But curiosity gets the better of me when I see two shadows. My heart thumps. Somebody's giggling. Christian and Mary are standing in the corner with wild hair, lips swollen from kissing, and red necks. My heart, which was pounding rapidly before, seems to stop. They hear me and pull apart—guilt's written all over their body language. I feel their eyes on my retreating back, but I keep walking with Vinny on my heels.

"Ann, I tried to warn you."

My face drops to my pillow the moment I enter my room.

Vinny obviously didn't want me to find out like this, and it's as though the words are being dragged out of him as he tells Karen, "Prince Christian was kissing Lady Mary in the hallway. I warned Ann not to go that way, but she didn't listen."

Karen has her hands on her hips, her expression murderous. I update them on this morning's kiss and how I thought the Prince and I had a mutual understanding. "I feel jealous and angry, when I should be happy and relieved that he has moved on." I rub the back of my neck as I replay the scene in my head. "I didn't realize seeing him with another woman would affect me like this."

I blow my nose and fix my makeup; then I eat my steak and mashed potatoes, resolute in my decision to not think about Christian and Mary. I give Karen a tight hug and make my way back to work with a newfound determination. I don't want to talk about it anymore but appreciate the support and kindness of my friends.

It's quiet in the office. It doesn't seem like anybody is back from lunch. I focus my energy into getting things completed. I run numbers and make to-do lists, and soon the volume of things done is greater than the number of things pending. I have been sitting in this chair all day and my butt is numb. The man I met at breakfast knocks on my office door.

"What can I do for you, Kevin?"

He gives me a mischievous smile, and I begin to think he's about to say something inappropriate when he asks, "Do you have the financial report for the building?"

"Here you go. And it includes labor and parts too."

"Well done, Ann. You work fast. I'm impressed. The Queen needs to approve the budget before we continue, but she's downstairs with Prince Ryan at the moment."

"That's great. I didn't realize he was back."

Kevin looks at his watch. "Well, I'm going home for the day. Unless you want me to take you out for dinner?"

"No, thank you, Kevin, but I appreciate the offer."

"Well, maybe a rain check. I may not be a Prince but I can still show a girl a good time. Have a good night, Ann. Don't work too late, honey."

I pour over the papers, running numbers and looking at the designs. Excitement rushes through me at the thought of seeing the chickens free and happy for the first time in their lives. They've never seen grass, trees, or felt the sunshine on their wings and I can't wait to see their reaction. Another knock pulls me out of my thoughts, and this time it's Ryan.

"Well, well, look what we have here. I was surprised when I heard about all the excitement. Leaving us and coming back as part of the team. You know how to make an impression." He grins. I jump up and we wrap our arms around each other. "Miss me?" Ryan asks.

I laugh at his question and pull away as the rest of the royal family walks in. The Queen says, "I'm sorry we left you to it, Lady Ann, but we had a surprise at lunch."

"No problem. I triple-checked the financial report and it's ready for your approval."

She beams at my progress. "Lady Ann, that is great. You are fast, and if your attention to detail is as thorough as the speed at which you work, then I made a sound business decision in hiring you. Forgive me. I am going to head to bed early tonight, but I will look at it first thing in the morning."

The King glares at his sons, conveying some kind of unspoken message, and walks out behind his wife with his hand on the small of her back, leaving me and the Princes alone. I cock a brow. "Your mom looks exhausted and your dad seems agitated."

Something passes between the siblings.

When nobody speaks, I target Ryan. "Did she catch you making out with Lady Mary too?"

He turns a laugh into a cough, but it's Christian who responds to my sarcasm. "I do not need, nor do I want to explain myself to the help. Remember who you are talking to and don't use that tone around me again. You are here because I have agreed to it. I can easily revoke your employment, and don't for one second think I won't have the Queen's backing if I were to press the issue," he hisses and brushes past Vinny as he goes.

I turn to Ryan. "He seems touchy tonight. He must be feeling guilty."

"I've bought something for you. But I left it in my room. Want me to go get it and bring it back, or do you want to come with me?" Ryan is quick to change the subject.

"Lead the way."

Ryan's room isn't as clean or well organized as Christian's. But it feels homier and he has drawings and notebooks on the desk, which shows that it's a workspace. It's lived in, whereas Christian's room is stark and — like him — all about show. I look at Ryan's drawings. He's a wonderful artist. Mostly focusing on landscapes and buildings.

"Close your eyes," Ryan asks with his hands behind his back. "Please? I didn't have enough time to wrap it."

I play along and outstretch my palms. He gives me a medium-sized box, and I gasp when I open my eyes and peer down at the brand-new, high-tech camera. "Ryan, it's beautiful. Thank you so much."

"Open it and try it out. It may not be any good. A camera is a personal thing, you know. It has to fit the photographer."

"Thank you, but I'm confident it will be a picture-perfect match for me." I watch his tired eyes. "Ryan, you look exhausted. Is everything okay?"

There's a knock at his door and Christian lets himself in, speaking without looking up, "Ryan, we…" He stops as soon as his gaze lifts to meet mine. Christian purses his lips. "Ryan, we need to talk. Privately."

His intrusion and demands for me to be dismissed, as though I'm someone without significance, is disrespectful. "Can you possibly give me a few more minutes with Ryan, Prince Christian?"

He glares at me, and Ryan reaches for my hand as a show of support. "Lady Ann, please give us a moment to talk. You should test out the new camera by taking some *before* shots of the chicken coop."

I push past Christian, slamming the door just enough to ensure my displeasure's known, and hear yelling from the other side almost immediately.

"Well, you move on fast! How dare you treat her like that."

"Me? What have I done wrong, Ryan? Ann and I are just friends."

Vinny speaks behind me, and I jump. "Are you ready for dinner?"

I look up sheepishly. "Thanks for that, Vinny."

"I figured that wasn't a conversation you'd be interested in."

After Vinny is gone, and it's just us girls, I explain the highs and lows of my day to Karen. She listens and rubs my back. "Ann, you have had quite the afternoon. I hope tomorrow goes better for you. Would you like me to order some food?"

"I am hungry, but I would rather change, go down to the servants' quarters, and eat with friends." I throw on a pair of jeans and a white t-shirt, let my hair down, and slip into my sneakers. Together Vinny, Karen, and I go for dinner.

It's weird sitting with Karen and Vinny in uniform while I'm in casual clothes. But I love the company.

I glance around and make sure we are alone. "Guys, please help me. I'm desperate for advice."

Karen starts cautiously, "Ann, you are wrapped up in our employers' lives. It's hard to ask for our advice and expect honest answers. We could lose our jobs."

Vinny sighs before adding, "Ann, you aren't their first choice. Tell them no and move on. You deserve better. Never accept anything less than a man who will put you first, choose you, and accept you for who you are and not for who they want you to be."

Karen pops a chip in her mouth. "I never realized you were such a romantic, Vinny."

"I am full of surprises, Karen." He sends a devious smile her way.

As we laugh, I release a breath and lean into my chair. I watch them banter back and forth about who's going to eat the last of the chips. If things don't work out for me at the Palace, at least I'll forever have these two in my life. And for that, I am grateful.

Confusion

I dress while humming a song my mother taught me when I was only knee-high and we would do our early morning chores together. Although the words are lost amongst the dust of my memories, the tune still brings peace to my heart. I sip my hot coffee and run a brush through my hair. Karen answers the door, expecting our breakfast, and backs up to allow Christian to pass. I continue my humming as Karen excuses herself and I wait for Christian to speak.

"I would like to have lunch with you today, Lady Ann."

I place my brush down and my heart rate increases. "How many women are you dating now? And yet you come to the one woman who's unavailable?"

"What do you mean *unavailable*?"

"Prince Christian, I'm sorry but I can't. I am very busy today. Is there anything else you need from me?"

He redirects his argument. "Lady Ann, I helped your farm and you gave me your word that you would share a meal with me. And I took you as a woman of your word. Would you please reconsider my offer?"

"You're right. I did give you my word when you helped me." I let out a breath. "Fine. I will accept your offer. However, let me make it clear that I'm accepting your offer only as payment due and for no other reason."

"Thank you, Lady Ann. I will see you later today." And he walks out.

I throw my body towards the bed in exasperation, miss it, and land on my butt on the floor with a loud thud. Vinny pops his head in with a worried look. He sees me and starts laughing. "Ann, are you okay?"

"Mentally or physically?" I grab his hand.

"The Prince was pretty mad. Is everything okay between you two?"

I'm unsure what to say. The exchange between us was awkward and not easy to explain, not even to myself. Thank goodness Karen comes in with breakfast and Vinny leaves. I eat my eggs, biscuit, and bacon quietly. Then I get ready to go to work, and when I arrive, I jump in and get busy. I'm determined not to let the dread over my lunch date overtake my mood.

The Queen comes to see how I'm doing. "Lady Ann, the finance report is approved, and we are ready to build. You have been allocated a budget to order supplies and get a bidding war scheduled for a contractor to start work as soon as possible. You can coordinate with our finance manager, Kevin, at your convenience."

"Now that the hard stuff is done, and the project is predominately outdoors, does this mean I can go back to wearing regular clothes and move into the servants' quarters?"

She laughs and pulls her reading glasses off. "Oh, Ann, I admire your spirit. I will make you a deal. You'll stay here, but you may wear casual clothes such as nice pants and shirts.

Unless you are working outdoors, then you may wear your jeans. Okay?"

I nod and take the approved report from her. Kevin is flirting with a blonde, as she laughs and bats her lashes at something he says. I clear my throat as I approach and she sashays away. "You move on quickly, Kevin," I tease.

"Prince Christian made it clear that if I wanted to keep my job, I was to stop pursuing you."

My eyes widen. What? Christian has no right to talk to Kevin about me or make choices on my behalf. It's none of his business.

"Great work today, Lady Ann. After lunch, we can start getting busy."

"Thank you, Kevin. I look forward to getting the ball rolling as quickly as possible." I turn to leave and see Christian in the doorway.

"Lady Ann, are you ready for lunch?" He looks at me, but I can tell he is warning Kevin with a glare.

"Yes, all set." I turn back to Kevin with a mischievous wink and add, "Thank you, Kevin, I will see you soon."

He noticeably swallows and walks off.

"Is that why you are unavailable, Lady Ann? You are interested in Kevin?"

"No. Kevin is just working with me for the time being."

Christian leads the way, expecting me to follow behind him like a subservient dog. I make a face at his back, and one of the servants sees me and turns a laugh into a cough. Then

I close the distance and pull up alongside the Prince. He takes me to one of the dining rooms and guides me by my waist, even when we pass the remaining girls in the competition. I blush as they glare my way. But he is unfazed and shuts the dining room doors behind us. The table is laid out with candles on a red tablecloth, and a carafe of wine sits beside a pair of long-stemmed glasses.

"This is beautiful, Prince Christian. You really shouldn't have gone through all this trouble," I say as I take a seat.

He sits across from me. "Would you like some wine?" He pretends to ask me as the butler is already pouring it.

"It's only lunchtime." I push the glass away. "And I am not a big drinker. I prefer coffee as my poison."

The butler drops off a salad and Christian and I eat in an awkward silence. After a few bites, I bring up just one of my many irritations. "Did you ask Kevin to stay away from me?"

He pauses mid-bite and shakes his head. "That is absurd. I merely asked him to not pester you or be a nuisance in any way."

I grit my teeth. "Why would you do that?"

He blots his mouth with his napkin. "Because I can."

I wait for more, but he doesn't say anything as he sips his wine with complete arrogance, so I press on. "I asked you why? And your childish response is hardly a proper answer."

He sighs and places his glass down. "Ann, Kevin has a reputation around here. He likes to date women, then he gets what he wants, and dumps them. I couldn't forgive myself, or him, if that happened to you."

I narrow my eyes. "I'm a big girl. I can take care of myself."

"Ann, you broke your ankle and can't walk past a pond without falling in."

"I hurt my ankle. I never broke it—and it was your brother who fell in the pond."

Our fresh Atlantic salmon arrives and I stab at it, imagining his face on my plate. When the dessert is brought out next, Christian seems to forget that he's punishing me with his sulking. "I don't like that you are unavailable to me, Ann," he says suddenly.

I allow my fork to glide into the chocolate cake and don't let him ruin the sweetness with his sour attitude.

When I ignore him, he stops eating and slams a hand on the table. "Who is it?"

"Why does it matter to you? We are just friends after all." My brow lifts.

"Because you are part of this process and you should not be dating. It's not permitted while you are working at the Palace."

I poke my fork in his direction. "You asked me to leave, which means I am free from the competition madness. I am an employee of the estate, hired on merit, and therefore free to do as I please." I've lost my appetite and push my cake away. "Well, this has been enlightening. Thank you for lunch."

"So, we agree then?"

"I think we agree that my *private* life is seriously none of your business. I have no interest in you, or these games that you are playing. If you wish to remain my friend, you will be wise to remember that."

As I storm out, Christian is behind me in two quick strides. He pushes me against the wall with his body pressing into mine. My heart pounds and my cheeks heat up. My breathing comes out in fast pants as I stare into his icy eyes. I swallow hard as I watch his lips.

"Why are you always so difficult?" He dips down to kiss me, but I squeal and slip past him.

"You told me you wanted to be friends, but you have made it clear that you only want a physical relationship with me. I'm not a toy you can play with, then cast aside. I'm a living, breathing person with feelings and needs too. Can you give me what I need? If not, then I suggest you leave me alone or I'll have no choice but to file a formal complaint against you and your conduct." I wish he would let me in and talk to me about what is holding him back. But he stays silent and shakes his head in defeat. "Of course not. I didn't think so. Please, leave me alone and stop trying to protect me."

I'm working in the office when Ryan comes around the corner. "Ann, I'm sorry about last night. I was tied up."

I raise a hand. "Please, Prince Ryan. I can't handle this right now. I accept your apology if you accept mine for being emotional. It has been a long week and it isn't over yet."

"I know what you mean. Even talking things over with Cherie went pear-shaped. She ended our relationship. Apparently, I'm *in love with you*. After all this time together, she doesn't trust me."

"But I hardly know you."

"I told her that and I tried to prove her wrong, but it didn't work."

"What are we going to do with ourselves? Maybe I can call her and explain everything?"

"I appreciate that, but I don't think she will listen to you." He stands and gives me a hug just as Christian comes in.

"What is going on? Every time I turn the corner, I see you two in some sort of embrace." He glares at us.

"Nothing is going on."

Ryan looks at Christian. "Does it really matter? Ann is working for Mom now that you dismissed her." A few people, including the Queen, have come back from lunch and are watching the brewing argument unfold between the two Princes.

Christian ignores them. "Maybe I will change that and add her back in."

"You would do that to her and the other girls?"

Christian lifts his shoulders. I go to walk out and leave

him with a parting shot. "Don't do this, Christian. You don't love me or want me as your wife. Just let me go."

Everybody is watching us and waiting for him to confirm or deny his affections for me. Emotions pass through his eyes. And he whispers softly so only I can hear, "You don't know that I do not love you." He's angry and yells at the onlookers, "Get back to work." They scurry away, whispering and grumbling amongst themselves. And I slip back to my work, but he stops me. "Not you, Lady Ann. We need to talk."

"All we do is talk; we go around in circles and nothing comes of it."

"I have been trying to speak to you, but you keep walking away."

"You have tried talking? No, you keep bottling things up and avoiding the situation by kissing your problems away." When he stomps off in response, I say to Ryan, "My life was far less confusing before I met you two."

He laughs. "But your life was also less exciting. Face it, Ann, you love us."

I smack him on the arm, fighting back a chuckle. "Shut it, you. Please, Ryan, let me call Cherie and explain."

"No, it is over. Two years of my life are gone because of a stupid rumor and her lack of trust. But thanks for trying. You know what, Ann? Even though you feel like your life is a mess, I'm glad you came. You are kind, caring, and one day you will make someone a wonderful wife." He smiles a sad smile and walks out of the office.

Troublemaker

The rest of the workday moves slowly. I focus on researching contractors for the up-and-coming bid. Growing up on a farm, we mostly did our own work when restoring or building an add-on. But every now and then, we had to hire help and some of the names on the list are familiar to me.

Vinny pops his head in. "Lady Ann, I was asked to escort you to the throne room by Queen Elizabeth."

I put my head on the table and bang it with a thud. "Why does she want me? What if I refuse?"

He responds less formally and in a lower tone, "Adulting is hard work, Ann. The way I see it you have two options: either you can run from it, or deal with it. But if you run, you need to know I was a great track and field athlete, so you don't stand a chance of getting away."

"And those are my only two options? Can't I just make it all go away?"

He laughs and shakes his head. "You are not a quitter, Ann."

"But I would really like to be one today." Uncertainty closes around my throat and makes it hard to breathe. I take in a deep breath and hold my head high. Once I'm standing at the throne room door, I decide to clear up one small point. "Are you positive I'm not a quitter, Vinny?"

"Absolutely," he says with a wink.

The King, Queen, and Prince are all waiting for me. "Lady Ann, thank you for joining us," the King addresses me,

91

and I squirm. "It has come to my attention that you do not want to be a part of the selection anymore. A process, I remind you, that you volunteered for willingly. Is this true?"

"My King, you are right. I did willingly sign-up and participate, but Prince Christian eliminated me from the competition. With all due respect, your majesty, my employment and position here have nothing to do with Prince Christian as I was hired by Queen Elizabeth and just wish to do a good job for you and my country."

The King takes this in and the Queen smiles reassuringly. He rubs his temple and looks back at me. "Lady Ann, are you willing to rejoin the selected girls?"

I can see Christian watching me from my peripheral. Am I? Can he ever open his heart to me? Will he ever actually choose me? I think back to our first kiss. He was caring and gentle. But did I imagine that man?

And then there's Ryan and everything he has lost because of me. The jealousy that Christian displays as well as his attempts to keep Ryan and me apart...

"Prince Christian, did you lie to Cherie? Tell her that I was involved with your brother?"

His eyes dart to his dad and then me, before he stammers out, "I may have spoken to her and your name may have come up in conversation, though I don't remember the exact nature of our discussion."

The Queen is displeased. "Christian? Why would you do that to Ryan and Cherie?"

He doesn't answer his mother at first and shuffles his feet. He is jealous and willing to play dirty to get what he wants. That includes hurting his flesh and blood. "I am not sure why I did it. I am sorry." Then he looks at me with something that resembles humility and honesty. "Ann, please tell me what I can do to give us another chance."

He is tortured. I care about him and hate seeing him so broken, but I don't think I am the healer he needs. However, maybe I can fix one relationship out of this mess. "I would like an apology. Not only to me but to your family. You hurt us and you ruined a two-year relationship. Please call Cherie and explain everything to her. Ask her to forgive you for your actions and take your brother back."

"I think Lady Ann is right," Queen Elizabeth adds.

The King is a man of few words and hasn't said much. For the most part, he allows his wife to tow the Prince back in line. However, he is annoyed with the fighting between his sons and is ready to apportion blame. "I do not want Lady Ann here. She is a bad influence on the Palace and has turned our sons against each other. I would like her to leave. Christian has never behaved like this before. This competition opened with ten contestants and the only name I hear repeatedly is Lady Ann."

Why is he blaming me for everything?

But the King hasn't finished his tirade. "I think it would be best if you went home." He turns to the Queen. "We don't need her for the project, and we have two lovely girls left for Christian to choose between. And neither of them are causing a scene."

The Queen tries to pacify him. "But, dear, the other girls are only interested in dresses and crowns—Lady Ann has proven herself willing and able to work. Please reconsider and give her a chance. She is a challenge for our son, and I think having a spirited girl rather than just the average, empty-headed prospect is admirable. The reason you have heard Lady Ann's name is because she stands out amongst the other contestants."

"Seriously, Elizabeth? She is more trouble than she is worth. Why can't you see that?"

I wish I was invisible. How did I become enemy number one in all of this? I stand with my chin raised. "My King, I am sorry for the trouble I have caused you and your family."

Christian slumps in his seat. I feel for him, but I am not going to argue with the King. The Prince chooses to address his mother instead, "Mother, this is all my fault, but I can fix it. Lady Ann is not to blame. She is doing some amazing work with you, right?"

The Queen nods in agreement. "You are right, Christian. Lady Ann has been extremely helpful. She is smart, motivated, and a hard worker. It will be challenging to complete this project without her."

The King groans and kneads his temples. Then glares at me as if I were an annoying bug on his windshield. "Fine.

Lady Ann may stay." The King turns to Christian. "But no more fighting or scheming to get your way, young man, or so help me, you won't need a chauffeur. I will drive her home myself."

The Queen smiles and follows the King out of the throne room, leaving Christian and me alone. I hear him kick a chair across the space and pivot to face him.

"What have I done? I have made a mess of everything. I cannot be a King when I can't even run my own life. Look at me." He leans against the wall and slides down to the floor, his hands raking through his hair.

"Thank you for standing up for me. It was nice hearing pleasant things about myself for once."

"You are thanking me after all this? If you do want to go home, I understand and won't try to stop you."

I laugh. "You worked so hard to get me to stay and now you want me to leave." I tap my shoulder against his.

"I just want you to be safe and happy. I know I go about things the wrong way, but that's all I've ever wanted— for you to be content. And that thing with Lady Mary, well, I suppose I wanted to make you jealous. I was angry and wanted to hurt you like I was hurting."

Since he is being so open, I decide to take a chance. "Christian, may I ask you a question?"

"Yes, anything if it makes you stay."

"Why did you send me home if you wanted me to remain in the competition?"

"It is complicated. I didn't have a say in it. I knew you didn't want to be here. I could tell you were not happy, so I sent you home."

"And what about our kiss?"

"We have a connection, Ann, but if you do not want this life, I can't get serious with you. Then I saw how you took charge. How you accepted a job here and you looked comfortable and happy. I was confused because if you hated being here so much, no salary or job opportunity would have lured you back. It made me think that I was wrong, and that you do fit in here. That you would make the perfect Queen." He sighs. "Then, when I kissed you, you told me to stop. You said you were unavailable, and I feared I was too late, and it scared me."

I take in what he has said. "Your mom is a remarkable woman and has some big shoes to fill for whomever you choose."

He laughs at my honesty. "My mother is great, isn't she? But, Ann, you are too. You want to change and improve lives, right?"

I blush. "I will give it another try."

"And I will try to fix this predicament I have created with Ryan and Cherie." He squeezes my hand. We share a rare moment of vulnerability and understanding. He moves close to me and my breath catches, my lips expecting a passionate kiss; but instead, he puts a soft kiss on my cheek and pulls me to my feet. "I would like to give you more, if only you would allow me."

"I would love nothing more than to kiss you, Christian. But I need time. I still can't get you and Lady Mary out of my head." I touch his face and feel new stubble growing in. He leans into my hand and then kisses my palm. Fire runs up my arm and I pull away. "Are you hungry?"

It takes him a second to process my question. He blinks, looking at his watch. "It is getting late, isn't it?"

"I could make you dinner and show you where I like to hang out? It won't take long and, in the meantime, I'll shower and change."

"That sounds nice. I will meet you in your room in half an hour."

Dating

I can't imagine Christian even owning a pair of jeans. This man needs a lesson on how to relax and enjoy the simple things in life, and that's my goal tonight. I know it won't be an easy task, but I'm up for the challenge.

Vinny pulls me out of my thoughts. "I overheard the King and Prince arguing. What's going on?"

"The King doesn't like me living within the Palace walls and is blaming me for the fights between the Princes. And Christian explained things to me and apologized. We have stuff to work out, but I won't give up on him just yet. I want to see where this goes. Plus, agreeing to give us another try may gain Ryan another chance with Cherie. And he ought to have that and more. Considering Christian was basically the one who broke them up."

Vinny smiles as he opens my door for me. "That is very considerate of you, Ann. And you wanted to quit."

"Go change and meet us in the break room. I don't think you lurking around in the shadows is going to help me right now." I smirk, then rush to catch up with Karen as I change.

"Ann, that is great news. I will help you however I can and get you back in the game."

"Karen, there is no game. I'm not competing with the other women. I'm either good enough or I'm not." I pull on my jeans and t-shirt, and she wrinkles her nose.

"You are wearing that? Shouldn't you be trying to impress him?"

"I love these." I sigh. "Karen, he needs to love me for who I am. And this is who I am, jeans and all. Besides, I am comfortable. Are you ready for dinner?"

"Me? What do you mean?"

"I am going to the break room to eat with Prince Christian. I'm taking him out of his element and teaching him something new. He doesn't know what we are doing yet, but it will be good for him to eat with me in my workplace. He is a Prince, but it doesn't mean he can't break bread with his employees. If he's going to choose me, he needs to know what he's getting, and our relationship needs to be built on compromise as well as new ways of doing things. He's out of touch with the people and I want to get him to relax and be comfortable. Do you want to come? Vinny will be there too." I apply clear lip gloss.

"That is an interesting tactic to take, Ann. If Vinny will be there, I guess I have to keep him from becoming a third wheel. But I must warn you: the Prince is not going to like being around his employees and there may be discord."

I brush my hair and throw on my white sneakers. This is how it should be. No pressure, no worries, just letting your hair down and having dinner with friends.

A few minutes later, I smile at Christian's clothing. He's wearing nice dress pants, a button-up shirt, and dress shoes. "Is this close enough to jeans for you?"

I undo the first two buttons of his shirt and lay my hand flat on his bare chest. His eyes light up at my touch and I feel his heartbeat quicken. "We need to buy you some jeans."

"Ann, I'm famished," he announces, staring into my eyes.

I blush and turn to Karen. "We will meet you there."

"I thought we were eating alone?"

"I wanted you to meet my friends."

"Friends? I thought they were your servants?"

I laugh. "Can't they be both?"

He wrinkles his nose in response.

We make it to the break room as Vinny is unloading the lunchmeat, cheese, and condiments from the fridge. He nearly drops everything when he sees me with Christian. But quickly recovers and smiles. "Good evening, Prince Christian. Lady Ann."

I laugh at his reaction and go over to help him.

"Can I be of any assistance?" Christian offers awkwardly. He's never mingled amongst the servants before and is uncomfortable with the prospect. Karen and Vinny are my friends, and they will always be my friends first and Palace employees second. Christian needs to accept that now and we have to find a way for us both to be easy with it.

"Thank you." I pass him the condiments and we set up a station for everyone to make their own sandwiches.

Karen arrives in tight jeans and a red tank top. She has brushed her hair out and put on some makeup. She appears to be on a mission of her own.

"What took you so long?" Vinny teases her as he takes a seat next to Christian, while Karen seats herself next to me and sips her soda.

"So, Lady Ann, what are your weekend plans?" she asks.

"I would like to visit the barn and flower gardens with a good book. I heard the roses are in full bloom and they have almost every color imaginable."

"That sounds incredibly relaxing."

The silence is awkward, and I feel the tension and unease building. "Christian, how is your sandwich?"

"Good, thank you. And how is yours?"

"Good, maybe too much mayonnaise but good."

Vinny pats his mouth with a napkin and leans back. "Prince Christian, I'm putting my neck out there. But as we're eating together all friendly like, I was just wondering: what are the odds of Ann being the one you marry?"

We nearly choke on our food. But Christian recovers fast. "I am not sure that is any of your business." He sees my silent warning, my expression cautioning him to play nice, and alters his tone. He's trying hard—bless him. "This is a new experience for me. And to be courting so many women at once is overwhelming. They each have their own unique qualities. I am exhausted. And everyone has an opinion as to whom I should and shouldn't choose. With this in mind, no matter my decision, I'm going to inevitably hurt someone's feelings. Marriage is challenging as it is and trying to combine two completely different lifestyles is hard. Hence the reason I'm here, with you, doing… *this.*" He lets out a breath.

"Amen, brother." Vinny raises his glass. We all laugh and relax at his honesty. Then he side-eyes me and Karen. "Women are the worst, Prince Christian. At least with a man, you know where you stand."

"Hey." I throw a chip at him.

"See what I mean? And I didn't even mention how wasteful they are."

We laugh again and assist him with clearing the mess. Once we are done, I move to the television and turn it on to see what movies are available. Christian sits on the couch next to me and Vinny and Karen sit on the opposite sofa. I flip through the channels and perk up when I find a favorite.

"Really? *Charlotte's Web*?" Vinny groans.

"Hey. My date, my choice. Suck it up, buttercup." I sit closer to Christian and he wraps his arm around my shoulder.

As we watch the movie, other servants move in and out of the room, oblivious to their Prince's presence. I smile up at Christian as he focuses on the screen in front of him. It feels nice to be doing something normal together. By midway through, I doze off and hear him calling my name.

"Ann?" he whispers, shaking me gently.

"Hmm?"

"The movie is over."

Vinny and Karen are gone. I yawn and stretch out. "Sorry about that. Did you like it?"

"I did. But I think I would have enjoyed it more as a child."

"Hey, it's a classic. Do you want to walk me to my room?"

He smiles and pulls me close. "Do I get a good night kiss?"

"I will take your request into consideration."

He grabs my hand and leads the way.

"Where is Karen?" I ask when we enter my room.

He closes the door behind us and laughs. "Well, she and Vinny got close during the movie."

"What do you mean? They were always close."

"They were making out."

"No. Are you sure?"

"Well, the lights were out, and it was dark but there was definitely some kissing. I can sit here with you until she returns if you want?"

"No way. You have some apologies and a phone call to make first thing in the morning."

"So, no good night kiss?"

"Fine, but just a little one."

He rubs his thumbs over my lips and I wrap my arms around his neck. We lean into the kiss, and when our lips touch, it is hard to remember the *little* part. All the passion and heat come back full force.

I'm not sure how much time passes because the world feels like it should. No worries. No protocol. No second-guessing. We are one.

"Ann, I missed your passion."

"You got a lot more from Lady Mary."

"You are two vastly different individuals. Mary tries too hard to get my attention. It's a chore keeping each other interested. Whereas you don't need to try. You always have my attention. And keep me on my toes."

"I wish you would choose already."

"I know, Ann. But this is a monumental decision and shouldn't be taken lightly." He kisses my forehead. "Good night, Ann."

"Good night, my Prince."

Karen comes in ten minutes later. My hands go to my hips in mock mother hen mode. "I fall asleep for thirty minutes and you and Vinny make out?"

"I blame you. All that talk about love and romance... And he really is an amazing guy."

We laugh and sit on the bed, talking about boys well into the early-morning hours. And my heart swells at the turn of events for us both.

Learning to Share

After that kiss, my dreams are consumed by images of our future. One filled with chickens and children running in open fields, laughing wildly.

When I wake, there's a tray of breakfast pastries and a coffee thermos on the side table with a note from Karen, saying she and Vinny went on their first official date and that she would see me later with details. I run my finger over her heart drawing on the back of the paper with a large V and K in its center.

That would be nice. To go on a real date, away from the Palace. I snack, drink my coffee, and have a bath. Just as I step into the hot bubbles, there's a knock at my bedroom door and I curse under my breath.

"Ann, are you in your room?" Christian calls to me.

"I'm in the bath. I'll be out in a minute." Then add playfully, "You know, if you chose me, you could be in here too." And I splash around so he can hear what he's missing.

He laughs. "I wish I could."

"Would you like me to wrap up my bath and put my clothes back on?"

"Yes, please do that. I will wait out here for you." I hear my bed creak. "Can I look through your belongings?"

"Sure." I have nothing to hide from him, except for some cute bra and panty sets. I drain the water and slip into my comfortable jeans and t-shirt. I exit the bathroom, towel-drying my hair as he's shuffling through my photo albums.

"Ann, who is this woman?"

I gently take the picture from his hand. I look down and run a finger over her face. "My mother."

"She looks like you. Do you have any more pictures of her?"

"No. She got sick shortly after that photo was taken. And she never recovered from it."

"I am so sorry. I did not realize..." He grabs another picture—one of me and Ryan this time. "I am glad I can make you smile like this too."

"There are other things you do to me that he doesn't."

"Anyone else make you feel that way?"

I think about it for a second. "I have little experience with men. I have always prioritized my dad and the farm. So, you are the only one. So far, anyway."

He laughs. The Prince is finally learning to lighten up with me. "And I hope I will be the only one. I apologized to everyone and called Cherie to explain the situation."

"How did that go?" I grab my camera, hoping to add some pictures to my collection.

"Cherie gave me a hard time but she calmed down when I told her I did it because you drive me crazy. She thanked me and promised to consider what I said."

"Maybe we could visit her and explain everything in person? Or we could invite her here and have a meal with them. A little bit of matchmaking never hurt anybody."

"I cannot leave the Palace. Even if I could, she still may not take Ryan back or even listen to what we have to say."

There is a knock on the door, and I call out, "Come in."

Lady Mary is dressed in a light-blue gown, sapphire jewels, and high heels. Her golden hair and makeup are perfect. I glance down at my jeans.

"Good afternoon, Lady Ann. How are you?" She walks into my bedroom with a smile, as though she has every right to be here, her stride nearly as graceful as her posture.

"I'm good, Lady Mary," I stutter. "May I ask as to what I owe the pleasure?"

"I was told Prince Christian was in here, Lady Ann. It's him I've come to see." Her impeccably painted lips curl. "Prince Christian, have you forgotten our lunch date?" She bats her eyelashes and lifts her chest.

"My apologies, Lady Mary. I must have lost track of time." He extends his arm for her to grab, and my stomach tightens as I see how perfect they look together. He turns to me. "Lady Ann, will you be available for dinner tonight?"

"I might be. Although I am expecting a call from my father and I may meet up with Karen and Vinny later. I was going to ask you to join us, but I see you're otherwise engaged."

Lady Mary is smug with the knowledge she could likely get two dates in one day.

I need a friend to vent to, and not knowing where to find Karen, I go in search of Ryan. I am surprised to see him in his pajamas when he answers his door. "Ann, what are you doing here?"

"I came to see if you wanted to help break in my new camera." I look down at his attire again. "Are you okay?"

"I just do not see the point." And he flops on his bed.

"The point? The point of what? It's just a few pictures."

He tosses a pillow at my face. "Not that. Life. In general. It never seems to go my way."

I toss the pillow back at him. "Oh, we're having a pity party and I didn't even bother to dress for the occasion. Let me check: you have a family who loves you, a mom and a dad, food on the table, clothes on your back, and best of all, a friend who is going to give you crap for the rest of your life for those awful pajamas." I wrinkle my nose at him.

"They are comfortable."

"Ryan, get changed and stop being depressed over a girl who cannot see how strong and *old* you really are," I tease.

"Is Christian okay with us taking pictures together? I can't face another argument with him. Especially after his heartfelt apology."

"What is that supposed to mean? Christian knows we are friends. And he is busy with Lady Mary."

"I don't know. My brother is quite jealous, and he apologized only last night. I doubt he miraculously feels better about us hanging out together."

"Okay, I understand. You probably can't handle all that sunshine anyway, old timer." I leave Ryan to his misery and make my way outside.

The fresh air reminds me of home, and I feel my tears welling up. I have given up so much. My family, my farm, my chickens, and now my friend. It doesn't seem fair. What has Christian had to sacrifice in his pampered palace life? I sit by the pond and wipe my tears away as the fish dance beneath the water's surface.

"This place brings back memories," Ryan says from behind me.

I turn to see him watching me. "Thank you for dragging this old man out of the house. And out of those pajamas."

"That's what friends are for. Speaking of, is it safe to ask about Cherie?"

He rubs his face. "We talked, and she told me not to expect anything, but she is going to come and visit soon."

After we stroll through the fragrant gardens, we make our way to the chicken house. I take some pictures of the exterior and surrounding areas, giving Ryan his space while enjoying the new camera and all the stylish features it has to offer.

"So how is everything going?" he asks, interested in the new coop plans.

And I'm more than happy to share my dream with him. I point out where everything will go and how the nesting boxes will be installed.

"What is a nesting box?"

"They are little boxes where the chickens can come and lay their eggs in privacy."

"They are smart enough to know where to lay them?"

"Of course, they are." I remember Pecker's hidden nest. "Some of them, anyway. Have you ever had fresh eggs that are still warm from the chicken?"

"Maybe? I never cook so I am guessing not."

I take a few freshly laid eggs and pull him towards the servants' break room. "Better late than never."

"Good, because I am starving."

I scramble the eggs while he sets the table. Soon, we have a meal made of toast and fresh eggs.

When we finish, he says, "That was incredible. Although I don't know if I can taste the difference. Thank you. I have never been in here before. I like the setup."

"It's my escape from the Palace madness. It's usually quiet, and everyone is nice."

Ryan has a sad expression etched on his face. "You do know that Christian cares about you?"

"Ryan, it's so complicated, and I don't know if I can trust him to be honest with me."

"Our lives are just as complicated as anyone else's. Even if you don't trust him, you can trust me, right? Those other girls do not stand a chance against you. He's going through the motions because he has to. It's his duty. Could you imagine what the press would do to us if they thought the competition was rigged? And because he's a man of honor, he can't tell you that. Don't judge him too harshly. He is a good man."

"I feel happy when I am with him and I know he feels it too. Then I see him act the same way with Lady Mary and it drives me crazy. It makes me question myself and our relationship. Maybe he is playing with me, keeping me around as a backup, and will let me go soon."

"What if he does, Ann? In life, we have choices to make and chances to take."

"What do you mean?"

"Listen: you are strong, proud, and kind. You can meet another guy and move on. Maybe somebody less complicated."

"Sounds like you need to take your own advice."

"Maybe you are right. But Cherie is giving me a chance, so I am taking it. At least until she says otherwise, because I am all-in with our relationship." He looks to me. "Are you doing the same?"

Am I really all-in? Can I push my jealousy aside and let understanding and patience take its place?

"I'm afraid of getting hurt."

"We all are, Ann, but that is part of the dating process. Part of finding our soul mates. For me, Cherie is worth the pain. Which is why we—you and me—cannot do this anymore."

I blink. "What do you mean?"

"Cherie has made it clear that she does not want me to be friends with you. If we are going to get back together, I can't even talk to you outside of normal interactions and discussions. I know once she meets you, she will love you and understand our relationship. But, for now, this is the way it has to be, and I hope you can understand and forgive me."

"So, you are sacrificing our friendship for Cherie?"

"Ann, I've invested two years of my life with her. Our families are connected, and the King wants her to be my wife. Even as the second son, I have a duty too, you know."

"But what about love, Ryan? Where does that fit into the Palace protocol?"

I hear laughter from the path, and Ryan doesn't have a chance to answer me. Vinny and Karen are holding hands and smiling as they stroll in.

Ryan stands. "Well, I should go. Thanks for your help and the meal."

I watch him walk away and grieve the loss of another friendship.

"Was that Prince Ryan leaving just now?" Karen asks.

"Yes."

"Where is Prince Christian?" Vinny looks around.

"The Prince is with Lady Mary today. Apparently it isn't my turn to play the girlfriend."

Karen hugs me. "I am sorry I was away all day."

"It was your day off too. Don't worry about me." I sigh. "Ryan told me he can't be friends with me anymore because of Cherie. She has forbidden it. What kind of marriage will that make?" I grumble to my hands.

Karen touches my arm. "We are here for you whenever you need us."

"Thanks, guys. I am going upstairs to read and escape for a while. You know what they say: boys are better in books."

Christian's Choice

Ryan is right. *I will survive.* I walk a little taller with this knowledge. Out of the corner of my eye, I see the King leafing through documents. "Are you and Christian arguing once again? It really is tiresome, you know. And it's not seemly for a Prince to be fighting with outsiders."

Taken aback and a little scared of his tone, I squeak out, "My King?"

"Christian is in a foul mood and I suspect you have everything to do with it, as usual."

"I am sorry, my King."

"Do not be sorry, Lady Ann. Just fix it before I fix it for you."

I take my leave and immediately go to Christian's door. I hear yelling on the other side, and I say, "Christian?" before grabbing the knob and pushing it open.

He turns to his butler. "You can leave, Jerry." And The man quickly scurries past me.

"Ryan's not even allowed to speak to me," I blurt out, on the brink of tears. "I don't want to lose him as a friend."

"I know. It was a part of Cherie's agreement to come here. Personally, I don't see a problem with that. Whether you meant to or not, Ann, you came between their relationship. And if they have a chance to fix it, you need to do the right thing and step aside." He huffs before adding, "How many friends do you need anyway, Lady Ann? First you buddy up

114

with the hired help, now with my brother. Why don't you ask the man who delivers the fish to break bread with you next? When is it going to end?" When he glances at my tears, he softens his tone. "You should not be so upset about the arrangement, considering it is what Ryan wants. If friends are so important to you, then his happiness is priority, right?"

"But what about my happiness?"

"That is why you have me."

"But you have other girls you are trying to make happy too."

"That is part of me selecting a future wife. It has been the same process for hundreds of years and has never failed."

"It doesn't mean I have to like it." I jump off his bed. "You are jealous of your brother and me, but we are just friends and have never proved otherwise. Imagine seeing us make out, having our hands all over each other, and you are supposed to be okay with that? Channel those emotions and try to put yourself in my shoes, Christian. I must suffer and see you with other women, even though you say you want to be with me. It hurts and is confusing."

He crosses his arms over his chest. "If you cannot handle that, then why are you here?"

"Christian, you begged me to come back, remember? I am here to try to be your wife, and I know it isn't easy for you. I will try my best to bite my tongue and be more understanding because I am all-in. I just need you to acknowledge my feelings and be patient with me."

115

"You're all-in?" he asks.

"Yes, I can't promise perfection, but I can promise to try."

"And what if I choose someone else?"

"I will find someone cuter and a heck of a lot nicer."

He looks away. "I bet that won't be too hard for you. I want the absolute best for you, Ann. Even if that means a life without me. I hope you will always know that, no matter what happens."

I take a step back. "It sounds like you have already made up your mind."

"I'm sorry, Ann. But, having weighed my options, I think Lady Mary is the best choice."

After everything we've been through, I am appalled. I feel betrayed and struggle to keep my temper at bay. I want to punch him in his smug face. And then kiss him to make it better. "Why?" The one word is all I can manage to say.

"Lady Mary is what I was expecting in a wife. She is the safe choice for our next Queen. She's predictable and controls her emotions. Ann, I am sorry I wasted your time. You are a wonderful woman." He runs a hand through his hair, searching my eyes. "Ann, please say something."

"Go to hell."

"Ann, please."

I raise my chin, forcing back the tears. "I hope you and Lady Mary have a wonderful life together." I try to walk past him.

"Is that all you have to say?" He stands in my way.

"No. Prince Christian, please kindly move so I can leave." I poke my finger into his chest. "You keep me here and beg me to stay, demand I avoid other men, and then you announce your engagement to Lady Mary? And that is *after* I tell you I am all-in for you. Give me a break. Something is wrong here. You cannot want this. You can't want me to leave after everything." My tears fall and I can't stop them.

He wipes them away. "Ann, you are one of the most intelligent and strong-willed women I have ever met." Then he bends his face and kisses me gently before pulling away to let me pass with a soft whisper of, "Goodbye."

"Prince Christian asked me to check on you and bring you something to eat," Karen says softly several minutes later.

"I'm not hungry," I mumble from under my pillow.

"Do you want to talk about it?"

"Not yet, Karen. I just want to be left alone. Please."

"I am here for you if you need me, Ann. You are not alone."

The next morning, I throw my pillow at the open curtains and nearly jump out of my skin when I hear somebody clear their throat. Christian is sitting quietly in my room, reading a book as though it's a library. "Karen said you are not talking to anyone or accepting any meals."

I roll out of bed and go to the bathroom. I take my time. As I exit, I turn the corner and nearly collide with a body.

Christian stands in front of me and I can feel heat radiating off his chest. I look up into his blue eyes. "Christian, I appreciate you taking the time to check on me. But we said our piece last night. It's over. You chose Mary. And once my project is done, I will be out of your life forever. You two can live happily ever after."

"This is hard on me too, Ann. You know that, right?" He grabs my chin and lifts it upwards.

"You have women at your mercy, all waiting for you to choose one. Choose them. And now that you have chosen, you get to live out your picture-perfect life. What's so hard about that?" I pull away from him.

"Ann, please. You know it's not that easy."

"Please, Christian. If you are happy with Lady Mary, then I am happy for you. But I'm sick of this hamster wheel and really do insist that you leave me alone this time. I'm not your plaything to be picked up and put down at will."

"I will be announcing my engagement tonight. I wanted to tell you in person so that it wouldn't come as a shock. There's no point in delaying it and I wanted you to hear it from me first."

My lip trembles. I wrap my arms around his neck and pull him against me. Our bodies burn as we hold each other tight. I am not sure how but we fall to the bed kissing. I try to pull away, but he tugs me to him and smothers my mouth with his urgency, his hands running up and down my frame and mine on his. I shiver as heat flows between us. Both of us want more but we know we cannot. I yank myself free of his embrace and roll from his grasp. "I am sorry," I say, near breathlessly.

"Ann, that was just as much my fault as yours." He fixes his clothes. I straighten my own disarray. "Mother wants a crowd for the announcement. Everyone is to assemble in the ballroom."

I nod my understanding, resolute in my decision not to sit around in my own misery, and head to the office to work. I write some reports and make to-do lists for tomorrow. Vinny approaches my desk, clothed in his formal uniform.

"Aren't you off today, Vinny?"

"Special event. I've been called into work. I'm sorry, Ann. I'd refuse if I could. I don't want to be there any more than you do."

I can think of nothing worse than attending the man I love's engagement announcement. So I speak to the Queen and ask to be excused. She's sympathetic but explains that, as one of the original contestants, I'm expected to attend for the official photographs.

Karen clears her throat as she brushes my hair later that night. "The King has requested that I move your stuff back to the servants' quarters while you are at the party." I force a smile and nod. "Good luck, Ann. I'll see you tonight." She hugs me tight.

I stare at my pink dress. It has a low back and V-neck and it fits like a glove. It's the prettiest dress in the wardrobe, and if I have to attend this farce, then I'm going to show the Prince exactly what he's lost.

The ballroom is decorated with white and blue streamers and balloons. The smell of fresh-cut flowers and fancy foods hits me as I enter. Christian makes his rounds and talks to everybody. I turn away as he pivots to look in my direction. I avoid him and run into Kevin from work.

"Hey, Lady Ann." He takes in my outfit and whistles, before offering me some champagne from a passing tray, and I accept it to keep my hands busy. "They have all of us office staffers sitting up here." Then he places his hand on the small of my bare back and escorts me to our seats. I'm not sure where my role lies tonight. Am I wearing my office worker hat? Or am I just a simpering contestant for the evening? I knock my drink back and grab another from the next tray that passes. It's fruity, bubbly, and helps my heart not ache so much.

At the table, I smile my widest smile and greet everyone, not realizing that Kevin's hand is still on my back until he moves it abruptly, and I see Christian towering over him. I raise my champagne glass in celebration. "Congratulations, Prince Christian." And I make a show of downing my glass in one go. The bubbles travel up my nose and I have to turn away as my eyes water. And this time it has nothing to do with tears.

"Thank you, Lady Ann. I trust that you are enjoying our fine champagne and that you will savor it this evening.

We are about to begin, and I believe you have been led to the wrong table." Christian lowers his hand to my elbow and leads me to the front with the other girls.

I drag my feet. "Boo, that was the fun table. Everyone likes me there," I pout, already feeling tipsy.

"Kevin is trying to get you to sleep with him, Ann."

I glance back playfully, my eyes landing on the man in question. "Really? Oh good. Do you think the party will let out in time for that?"

"Ann, stop this at once. And act with some decorum."

"Prince Christian, I'm a free woman after the announcement of your engagement to Lady Mary. The world is my oyster." I spread my arms wide to further emphasize my point.

"You and Kevin are not going to do anything of the sort."

"You are not the boss of me." I aim for another glass of alcohol, but the Prince stops me.

"I believe you have had a sufficient amount."

Okay, maybe he *is* the boss of me. I notice Mary watching us and elbow Christian. "You'd better hurry. Your fiancée doesn't look too happy."

The selected girls are sitting at the bottom of the prominent table beside the Royal Family, along with somebody who may be Cherie. She stares at me and Christian as we take our seats. The woman is very pretty with long black hair and dark eyes. I smile at her and she politely smiles back and inches closer to Ryan before taking his hand.

The Queen addresses the crowd. "I am glad to see everyone has made it to the party." She introduces us all to each other as a waiter pours more champagne for the table. I get a warning glare from Christian, but he can't say anything about it without causing a scene. And I can tell that, realizing I'm three glasses in, he's worried about what my comeback might be. I sip my drink, hoping it will not be a long night. The waiters bring out the food. We are served a fragrant roast duck with gravy, mashed potatoes, carrots, and fresh rolls. As we eat, I feel Christian's eyes on me, Mary is bristling, and I go out of my way to wind her up.

After the plates are taken away, Christian clears his throat and buttons his suit jacket. He stands, signaling silence around the room. He's a handsome and elegant man—I find myself thinking this as I watch him and can feel my heart swell. Despite the way it ended, I realize that I'm lucky I got to spend time getting to know him. He makes a short speech about how hard this has been for him and how lucky he (also) feels to be granted this opportunity to continue the tradition. He looks to each of us, thanking us for our attendance. He reaches me last, holding my gaze as he's talking to the crowd.

"So, without further ado, I would like to introduce my fiancée..." There is a brief pause as Mary beams up at him. "...Lady Ann."

For a second, I think I'm hearing things. Can alcohol do that to you? Mary turns red while Christian stares at her, not realizing his mistake until Ryan elbows him. There is silence until a ripple of nervous coughing encompasses the room. I look to Christian and our eyes meet. He glances at Mary as she pushes to her feet and storms out.

All eyes are on me and I can feel my cheeks brighten. I stare at Christian, willing him to say something to fix this, but he just stares back at me. "Christian, you said my name instead of Mary's," I whisper towards him.

And realization suddenly dawns on him. The King is red-faced and more aggravated than I've ever seen him. He's almost shaking with fury. Christian scrapes his chair back and the grating sound resonates around the room. He chases after Lady Mary and the doors, which have been held opened for the occasion and are flanked by two waiters, slam shut behind him. I look around, unsure what to do, while the awkwardness of the situation is drawing out into an interminable silence.

People are staring at me expectantly, as though I'm the one in charge. The one who is going to put this right. I take a deep breath and try to troubleshoot. When I stand, attempting to correct Christian's egregious mistake, there's a round of thunderous applause. I smile and wave. "Thank you, everyone. I appreciate your, uh, support. I hope that Prince Christian will return with his fiancée and clear up this embarrassing situation. But, for now, I think dessert is on its way."

Thank goodness the waiters get the hint and the trays come pouring out. A whisper of excited gossip flows with the double cream and I try to melt into my chair. I inhale, feeling sick and regretting the champagne. I poke at my cheesecake and keep my eyes open for Christian.

Ryan leans in and whispers to me. "Did he mean to call your name?"

"No, I don't think he did." I get up to find Christian. It might not be the best time to confront him, but I (more than anyone) have a vested interest in knowing what's going on. However, as I stand for a second time, everyone crowds around me to shake my hand and congratulate me on my engagement. I sway at the attention but manage to hold my own. As guests leave, I finally slip out.

Christian is in a hallway with his dad, and by the sounds of it, the conversation is not going well. I take a different route and sneak to my room. This is not my argument, it's certainly not my mistake, and the King will not appreciate my presence.

I fall onto my bed, exhausted, and Karen looks up from her reading. "So how horrible was it?"

"Horrible. So horrible that I do not know if I am single or engaged."

She laughs and brushes off my comment with a wave of her hand. "You are that drunk, huh?"

"Karen. Prince Christian said my name. Not Lady Mary's when he announced his fiancée. But he was staring right at her. It was so embarrassing."

She throws her book down and jumps up. "What?"

"Help me out of this dress and I will tell you everything."

A few minutes later, Christian barges in without knocking, and I smirk in his direction. "*Husband*, where have you been?"

"This is not funny. I have publicly humiliated my family." He paces the room. I have never seen him so distraught. "I messed up, Ann. I was so mad and thinking about you." He sits on the bed.

"Christian, I am sure you can fix this."

"As much as everyone would like me to be with Lady Mary, my heart belongs to you, Ann."

"Everyone? But this is your choice, right?"

"I told you that this is complicated."

"Does that mean we are engaged?"

"Let's sleep on it. We can figure out our future in the morning, okay?"

Karen jumps up when he leaves and squeals. "This is amazing. I cannot wait to tell Vinny—Ann?"

But I had already laid my tipsy head down on the pillow and was drifting off to sleep.

Epiphanies

I groan as Karen shakes me. "Time to get up, sleepyhead."

I toss the pillow over my aching head. "No. Five more minutes."

"Come on, I moved all your stuff. Now I just need you."

I try to ignore her as I continue to drool into my pillow. But then I hear a knock and a set of confident steps approaching and I know Christian is next to bug me. "I brought aspirin and coffee." He hands me the items. I do as I am told, then he scoops me into his arms. I screech at the sudden affection and hold on to his neck. "Karen, we will see you upstairs," he says over his shoulder, and she giggles.

He carries me past the servants and guards. Then he places me down outside the door next to his and opens it wide. The room is enormous. It has a queen bed, a couch, a TV, a dresser, end tables, a mini fridge, a desk, and a beautiful open balcony with a table and chairs set. I see pictures on the wall of me, my family, and chickens.

"Christian, this room is wonderful."

He shrugs. "I did some minor adjustments to make it feel like home. Ann, I know this is not exactly what you wanted." I run my hand over the soft bedspread and he continues. "Let me show you the best part." He opens a door. "It leads to my room."

I look around with many unanswered questions on my mind. Like: what happened to Mary? And how can he alter his decision so fast? But I push them aside and enjoy the moment. Christian chose me. Life is finally going my way.

"This looks like the start of a beautiful beginning," I say as I wrap my arms around his neck. I stare into his icy eyes. Although we had a bumpy start, I can't deny that I'm hopeful our friendship can morph into something wonderful.

After we've adjusted to the new arrangement, we each change, excited to get our day started. Karen assists me with slipping into a tight-fitting lavender dress with gold flecks. She places a glimmering tiara on top of my head and makes sure I look great. I meet Christian in the hall, and we hold hands as we go to breakfast.

"Ann, that crown suits you perfectly." He kisses my hand.

I feel the burden of the tiara weighing heavily on my heart, and my palms start to dampen. "Thank you, Christian."

When we take our seats, I see that we are the last ones to arrive. As breakfast is served, the King slams his newspaper on the table, making us all jump. I look down at the headlines. Front and center are pictures of us at the celebration last night and the caption questions who Christian actually chose.

I cringe as Cherie lets out a loud laugh and Ryan elbows her to stop. "This is great," she adds with a giggle.

Christian glares at Ryan, who shrugs apologetically and turns to his fiancée. "I wouldn't say it's great, Cherie."

"At least the attention is off us for a while." And she sinks her teeth into her pastry.

Thank goodness the Queen steps in gracefully and places a hand on the King's arm. "Dear, I am sure Christian can take care of the publicity concerning his engagement. Now please eat before your eggs become cold." Then she turns to me. "I got word this morning that the contractors are coming today to bid on the chicken coop and fencing."

"That is great timing. We just put the paperwork through."

"I told them you could meet with them this morning."

Christian frowns. "Can we give the outside work to someone else? Ann and I have things to discuss."

"Christian, it is very important to me to see this project through." I steady my voice.

"Well, it is for the best, Ann. You cannot be parading around in jeans and dragging filth all over the place. You have obligations and an image to maintain now."

I put my fork down. My face is red. He has never publicly degraded my clothes or work before. And I will not stand to be humiliated. "Christian, you knew who I was and what I did before you chose me." Then, as politely as I can, I excuse myself from the table.

When I enter the office a few moments later, I jump because everybody yells, "Congratulations." I smile and take hugs and handshakes from those around me. Then I grab the papers I need for the contractors before heading to my room to get changed.

Karen blinks at me as she adjusts my bedding. "Back already?"

I update her on my breakfast debacle. "I am just here to change. I have the contractors coming in to bid on the chicken coop work. I am meeting them outside to check out the area beforehand."

She helps me out of the dress. "I am sure Prince Christian was just stressed out. There is a lot riding on his shoulders."

"You are probably right, but he hurt my feelings, Karen. It was so degrading, hearing him say that about what I love to do." Then I slip on my jeans, boots, and a pink t-shirt and hope I am not late.

By the time I make it outside, Kevin is talking to the contractors.

"Good morning, gentlemen," I say politely as I greet the four men with clipboards. Then I turn to my coworker. "Hey, Kevin, aren't you a little out of your jurisdiction?"

"Prince Christian asked me to get the bids going, but if you would rather take lead, that's fine. Just remember to tell him it was all your idea, so I don't lose my head."

My eyes narrow. "Thank you, Kevin. I will take it from here."

He nods and steps aside. "As you wish, Lady Ann."

I show the contractors around and discuss our projected costs. I see them scribble their notes, and after we are done, they hand in their bids with smiles. I shake their hands and tell them I'll discuss the numbers with the Queen and get back to them as soon as possible. Doing any contracting work for the Palace is a great marketing tool for a company, and they're all eager to get the work. I expect some good prices. I leaf through the contractors' bids and they look great. Some are even under budget and prior to the deadline.

I change out of my muddy clothes and into a soft-blue dress with silver flats. I walk past Kevin's desk and see Christian glaring at him. He's clearly in trouble, but since he still has his head, I decide to brush past them.

The Queen looks up at my approach and I wave the papers at her. "The bids look very promising. I told them I would call them soon with your choice."

"That sounds wonderful. Thank you, Lady Ann."

Christian steps up beside me. "May we have lunch together?"

"I'm sure I can squeeze you in after I wash myself of the filth from outside."

Christian purses his lips and leads me to his room. He asks his butler to get us lunch. When Jerry closes the door behind him, Christian turns to me. "I thought when you said you were all-in, that it meant stepping up and acting like a Lady."

"You assumed a lot from those few words, Christian." I throw my hands in the air. "You knew I was a farmer from the beginning. That is who I am. I cannot change that. Nor can I keep repeating myself constantly until you get it through your thick skull. Why does it bother you?" My eyes are watery. "Why did you try to have Kevin take those bids for me when you knew how important it was to me?"

"Because I would rather you stay inside. I told you this at breakfast. Your role is inside the Palace. If you want to mess around in the office wing, that's fine, but I will not have you up to your eyes in grime—it's not what a Queen does."

"Christian, a marriage is based on compromise. It is not a dictatorship. I want to be with you, but I need you to accept me for who I am. Not who you want me to be. We've discussed this so many times and we keep coming back to this place."

Jerry enters with our meals, and for a moment, our conversation ceases, and we go to the balcony to eat.

I pick at my salad, my appetite all but gone. "Why can't you be proud of who I am?"

"I am proud of you, Ann. That is why I want to marry you. But farming is not a duty a Queen performs. She is a leader and a partner to her husband as he runs the country."

"This can't change or be modified, at all?"

He shakes his head, but I can't accept it.

"Do you realize all that I have given up being here, Christian? And the one thing I am asking of you is to give me a little compromise and allow me to work on this project. And keep the friends you insist on calling *the help*."

He raises his chin. "You knew what you were giving up when you came here, Ann."

"So, if I cannot change who I am, then I can never be your wife?"

"That is the case, yes."

I thought he came to terms with wanting to be with me because I made him happy. But he just wants me to change.

"I am sorry to intrude, Prince Christian, but your father called, Lady Ann, and he requests you call him back." Jerry bows slightly.

"Thank you for lunch, Christian, and the discussion. It was eye-opening as always."

Karen peeks up from her sewing as I stomp inside my room with Christian following close behind me. "Is everything okay, Lady Ann?" she asks.

I go to the phone on my bedside table. "I think something is wrong at home. My dad called the Palace and asked that I call him." The phone rings and goes to voicemail. "That's odd."

Christian frowns. "What do you think is wrong?"

I redial and it rings a few times. "Suzie? It's Ann. Dad called me. Is everything all right?"

"Ann, let me get your father."

I wipe the sweat off my forehead. "Dad, what's going on?"

"Ann, honey, I am afraid I have bad news."

I have a thousand scenarios running through my head. "Dad, just tell me what happened?"

"It's Pecker, honey. She's not doing well. I have tried every trick in the book, but I'm sorry... I know how much she means to you and I wanted you to hear the news from me."

I can't ignore my sudden overwhelming urge to go home and try to save her. I look at Christian. I know without saying anything that, to him, Pecker is just a hen. He'll say they have a hundred right here and to make one of them my pet, if I must have one. "Dad, I will see you and Pecker soon." I end the phone call before my dad can protest.

Christian appears mortified. "Ann, please, you cannot go right now. We need to work this out. You can't go home for a sick chicken. It's ridiculous."

"I'm sorry, Christian. But I need to go."

"Ann, please reconsider your decision."

I walk past him, choking on my emotions. Pecker cannot die without knowing how much I love her, not like Mom. As I round the corner, I run into Ryan. "Woah, Ann, where is the fire? Ann...? What happened? Why are you crying?"

I run past him too and down the stairs.

Ryan catches up to me, breathless. "Dang, you are quick. Now tell me what is going on?"

"How can I get a car?"

"Do you need to go somewhere outside the Palace? I guess we could use mine. Or I'm sure Christian can buy you your own."

"I need one now. My dad needs me."

"Ann, you're not in any state of mind to drive yourself. Can I call you a driver?"

"I don't know how long I will be, and I need a way to get back."

"Okay, calm down. I can take you to see your dad."

"Ann. Please wait up!" Karen shouts. "Prince Christian is terribly upset with the situation. He wants me to tell you to come back immediately." She takes a breath. "I'm sorry, honey, but he said to tell you that it's just a bird and to grow up."

"Tell him to go hang himself. He is insensitive to my needs and I am already driving away."

Karen hugs me. "Tell everyone at home I said hi. So sorry about Pecker, Ann. I hope that she's going to be okay. We will talk soon."

"Karen. Can you please inform Prince Christian that I am taking Ann, and he can call my cell phone? Also… maybe you could give me a head start before relaying that information?"

She laughs. "I will walk really slowly."

I turn to Ryan. "I don't want any more trouble. You should stay here. I can go home by myself."

He ignores me, takes his keys off a hook, and walks to a black Sedan with tinted windows. On the drive, I worry about my hen. I remember her as a fluffy chick, her first egg, and how big of a pain in the butt she is.

"Just go ahead and ask me already," I snap when Ryan keeps giving me nervous side-glances.

"It really isn't any of my business. But I'm worried about you, with your sick hen and the fight with Christian at breakfast."

"I'm grateful for your help and sympathy. Christian and I are always fighting because I am always doing something wrong." I swipe at my wet cheek. "What about you? Weren't you and Cherie on edge this morning too? Maybe it is just something in the air today."

He grips the steering wheel until his knuckles are white. "Actually, she left me shortly after breakfast. We are over for good this time."

"Ryan, I'm sorry. Do you want to talk about it?"

"No."

We drown in our shared self-pity for an hour before his phone rings. The caller ID says Christian is calling and I cringe. Ryan answers it with his steering wheel button. "Hey, Christian, you are on speaker."

"Ryan, you bring her back home immediately. Do you hear me? This is not funny. I am giving you a direct order."

I narrow my eyes at the phone. "Christian, I am driving now, and I do not intend on turning around anytime soon. I'm sorry.

"Ann, what are you thinking. I told you no. You have obligations and responsibilities here. You cannot just toss them aside and run off. And, on top of all that, you are taking Prince Ryan away from his duties without protection."

"First off, Ryan volunteered to drive me. I didn't force him. And you're right: this isn't funny. My beloved pet is dying, and I need to be with her. If you had even a speck of compassion, you'd understand. I know you are having a hard time, but please try to be kind, for me. The chicken that I hand-raised, myself, is in trouble. She needs me right now."

"Ann. Listen to me. It is an animal. They come and go all the time, especially chickens." I stay quiet and Ryan stares straight ahead. When the silence becomes too much, Christian continues in a determined voice. "Ann, I cannot do this. I have a press release in a few hours to announce my engagement and fix the media mess I made. And you are not here."

A tear rolls down my cheek. "Christian. Do you even want me there?"

He pauses. "No, I do not believe I do." He sighs. "I'm going to implore Lady Mary to come to the press release to announce our engagement."

I squeeze my eyes shut. I knew his answer before he spoke it, but it doesn't hurt any less to hear him verbalize it so casually.

"Ryan. Drive safe. Keep me updated on when you will be returning home. Goodbye, Ann. I wish you well."

Ryan glances over at me. "Are you sure you don't want me to turn around? Maybe you can still fight for him?"

I let his words roll over me as I consider my relationship with Christian. Do I want to fight for him? Of course, I do. But no matter how much I fight, it's never going to be enough. No, my fight is gone. I sigh and shake my head.

"Where are we going?" I ask as I look out the window.

"I'm starving. I could hardly eat breakfast with the tension at the table. Then Cherie left. And on my way to lunch, I ran into you. I will just grab a quick burger. Do you want anything?"

I shake my head and bite back a laugh. I cannot imagine a Prince using a regular fast-food drive-through, but he sure does. He orders a burger meal for himself, a milkshake, and extra fries. When we pull up and he rolls the window down to pay, my ears are bombarded with a high-pitched squeal from the blonde woman at the register. "Oh my gosh. See, Tiffany. I told you it was his voice." She bats her eyelashes. "Prince Ryan, it's so good to see you. You are much more handsome in person."

He smiles brightly. "Thank you." He reads her name tag. "Bonnie. How are you lovely ladies doing today?" he asks in a charming voice.

They giggle and five more girls crowd the space, each trying to squeeze through the window while a line of cars honks behind us. They pass him the food with napkins decorated with kisses and phone numbers.

"It is on the house, my Prince." Bonnie grins.

"I appreciate your hard work, ladies. Thank you again."

I laugh and toss a fry at his head. "I can't take you anywhere."

"What? Surprised by my charming attributes?" Ryan winks at me.

We drive to a quiet rest area, overlooking a retention pond. As we sit at a picnic bench, I look at my dress and his suit and snicker.

He hands me the milkshake and extra fries. "Good comfort food. It'll make you feel better."

"Thank you." I pull my tiara off and place it on the table. I let the cool breeze throw my loose hair around and moan softly as I feel the salty, warm fry make its way to my stomach. I tap his shoulder with mine. "How do you know this is good comfort food?"

Ryan stares at his feet. "Can you keep a secret?"

"Nope."

He laughs as he watches me. "I meet up with Bonnie after hours. I mean, she is so hot with her hair net and all. Plus, all the free fries a man can eat."

I roll my eyes. "Ryan, your dad would never let you date a cashier at a burger place."

He chuckles. "You are absolutely right. The truth is when mom is feeling under the weather, this is her go-to." He shrugs. "And she is a wonderful sharer."

"That is a lot more believable. Let me guess: it's part of her cycle food cravings?"

"Are all women like that? Do you have a special food you like?"

I lean back and sip my milkshake. "I like chocolate and greasy pizza."

"Hopefully not together." He wrinkles his nose.

"That's a great idea. I will have to try that next month."

After some food and getting out of my own head, I do feel better. I peek through my lashes at Ryan and wonder if he made that story up just to lighten my mood.

"What is going on over there?"

I look over and see a family of ducks waddling together. I watch as they plop into the sparkling water, one by one, and paddle away in a straight line. Then I glance in the direction Ryan is pointing. One of the yellow ducklings is quacking frantically at his family. An adult duck hears its cries and stops swimming to peck at a piece of plastic caught around the duckling's neck.

I push to my feet and Ryan grabs my arm. "Wait, Ann. What if the duck attacks you?"

"Are you afraid of a duck, Ryan?"

"No, of course not. I am only looking out for your safety."

"And I am looking out for the safety of a defenseless creature." I pull my arm away.

The adult pecks my foot and hisses as I near. The duckling tries to run off, but the plastic is relentless. I ignore the protests and collect the baby in my hands. I tug at the plastic and grumble.

"This poor duck is caught in somebody's garbage when there is a trash can right here. People are such assholes." Tears prick my eyes when the plastic doesn't loosen. "They never stop to consider how their actions have severe consequences for others." Even though I am glaring at the trash, I know my words are directed towards Christian and the way he has treated me.

"I don't believe it. Did you just curse? Lady Ann, that isn't very ladylike," Ryan teases. Then he slips two fingers between the plastic ring and the duckling's neck and tugs. The plastic snaps and falls to the ground. I kneel at the water's edge and set the bird down gingerly. The adult gives my arm a hard nip and takes off with the baby towards the others, all quacking and shuffling their tail feathers as they fade into the distance. "Ann, your arm is bleeding." Ryan searches the car for a bandage. "How about the napkins with the kisses on them?"

I push away his hand and search through my purse. I unwrap a panty liner and pat my wound.

"That's gross! Why would you use that?"

"You were trying to give me germ-infested napkins, and you think a clean panty liner is gross? You're jealous of my resourcefulness."

Ryan looks into my eyes. "No, you are wrong, Ann. I'm not jealous of your resourcefulness, rather it's your compassion for life that is truly admirable." Ryan's phone suddenly rings. The caller ID says Mom this time, so I relax and lean back. Ryan answers it. "Hey, Mom, you are on speaker. I am driving Ann home to be with her dad for a little bit."

"Thank you, Ryan, Christian brought me up to speed. Ann?"

"Yes, Queen Elizabeth?"

"I am sorry about your sick chicken, and about Christian's change of heart regarding the engagement. But I would like to remind you that we are working together, and I need notice when you leave."

"I'm so sorry, Queen Elizabeth. I was not thinking clearly."

"I understand. I am going to text Ryan the selected contractor's name and number, and you can call him at your convenience. I will see you when you get back. Ryan, be safe, dear. I am sure the press will be hounding Ann's father's house after Christian's press conference." There is a short pause, then she adds, "Ryan, I am sorry about Cherie. The fact that she was not honest with you is terrible."

"Thank you, Mom. Do you need us for anything else?"

"No, but I will be in touch."

I slowly turn to Ryan. "Did Cherie cheat on you?"

"Yes, that's why it was easy for her to break things off. Apparently, it was with a family friend she's always had feelings for."

"Ryan, I'm sorry."

"Me too. And I would rather not talk about it." We pull into my driveway and Ryan turns to me again. "Ready to go inside?"

Rough Day

I look up at my one-story, three-bedroom, two-bathroom, brick house and swallow the lump in my throat. Ryan puts a comforting hand on my shoulder.

"I am here for you whenever you are ready."

"Ryan, I just don't think I can handle losing two important things in my life. All in one day."

"Maybe you don't have to? And if you do, you will not be doing it alone."

"Dad, I'm here," I call out, as Ryan shuts the front door behind us, and Suzie tears up and smiles at me.

"Ann, look at you. You're absolutely breathtaking, dear."

"And who is this?"

I move aside so Ryan can come forward. "Prince Ryan." And he extends a hand to her as I ask, "Suzie, where is Dad?"

"He is with Pecker in the sunroom. Waiting for you."

My feet know the way, even if my heart screams no. My dad is kneeling on the carpet. By his side in a tote is my Pecker. Her chest is heaving as she tries to breathe. Her black eyes are half closed and tears well up in mine.

"Oh, Pecker." I stroke her black and white feathers. They feel rougher than normal under my hands. She makes a pitiful sound as she recognizes my voice. I grab her into a gentle hug and cry into her tiny body. "My sweet girl."

My dad offers a hand to Ryan. "Thank you for bringing Ann home. My name is Jack."

"It was my pleasure, sir. She was distraught, and I did not want her driving here alone. I am Prince Ryan, but please call me Ryan."

They give me a few minutes with her before Dad says, "Ann, honey, Pecker is in a lot of pain."

"Do you have any idea what is wrong with her?"

"I think she has an egg impaction. She is getting up there in age."

Ryan cautiously extends a hand and strokes her feathers. "I didn't know that could happen. How can we fix it? Laxative?"

My dad lets out a hearty laugh and I crack a small smile. "No, Ryan, I am afraid not. Unfortunately, we only have two options."

"Options are good, right?" He turns to me, but I cannot meet his gaze.

Dad rubs his stubble. "We can either let her suffer or put her down."

Ryan looks from Pecker to my dad. "You mean you can put her down with a quick shot?"

Dad places a hand on Ryan's shoulder and shakes his head. "Sorry, Ryan. It's never that easy."

I stare down at Pecker with silent tears falling as I stroke her. I feel Dad's strong arm around me, and I give him a short nod. I stand with Pecker in my arms, my skin bristling when I note how her bones are poking through her layer of feathers. "It is okay, girl. It's almost over."

"What is Jack going to do? Is he going to end Pecker's life? And you... you're going to watch?"

I return his gaze with a sad smile. "Ryan, she needs me. Even if it's uncomfortable to watch. I am not going to abandon her now. You can stay inside if you'd rather."

We go to the shed where Dad has an axe ready. I lay Pecker down on the log and kiss the top of her head.

"Goodbye, my sweet girl." I suck in a sob. "I will miss you dearly. Fly high with Mom." I take a few steps back and feel Ryan's warmth at my side.

The golden sun is setting and the orange and red rays smudge across the sky. My dad strokes Pecker and turns his tired eyes towards me. "Are you ready, Ann?"

I look down at Pecker and nod. Then I cling to Ryan. He wraps his arms around me as my dad brings the axe down. And Pecker is free of her pain and suffering.

I cry into Ryan's shoulder. Memories of Pecker pass through my mind. I am done having to say goodbye to the ones I love. He strokes my hair and holds me tight, allowing me to take comfort in his presence. Even with the warmth of the setting sun, I feel cold. Colder than I have felt in a long time.

Behind us, I hear a sudden rush of clicking noises and turn to see my dad stalking towards a flock of reporters. "Hey. This is private land. Get off my property." Then he turns to the Prince. "Ryan, can you get Ann inside while I run off the vultures?"

I am in a daze and not caring where I go. My girl is gone. I look down as I walk into the house and see red splatters on my dress. "Ryan, I need to shower."

His eyes drop to the blood stains. "Oh no, I am sorry, Ann."

We enter the main bedroom. I pass the TV and queen bed to grab clothes out of my dresser. Then I brush past Ryan as he glances around.

"You can wait in here if you want. Or the guest room and extra bathroom are down the hall."

"You have the main bedroom?"

"After my mom died, my dad thought I could use it more than he could. But I honestly think it hurt him to be in the same room they shared for so long."

"I cannot imagine how hard that was for him — or you. I can't envision growing up without my mother."

I walk towards the bathroom and turn to him. "Feel free to watch some TV or whatever you want. The remote is on the nightstand."

I blink at my reflection. My makeup is ruined, my dress is stained, and my hair is standing on end. As I run the hairbrush through my tangled nest, my mind wanders. Maybe that's how life works, with lots of knotted messes that you must work through until they're smoother.

I try to grab the zipper. And try again with no luck. I poke my head out of the bathroom. Ryan is lying on my bed with his shoes and jacket off, reading one of my farming magazines. I laugh at the absurd picture and he looks up.

"Ann, are you okay?"

"Ryan, has Suzie come inside the house yet?"

"Last I saw, they were barreling down the road after the reporters." He chuckles. "Your dad sure can run fast. Anything I can help with? I feel so useless."

I stare at him for a moment then turn around, moving my long hair aside, and point to the stubborn zipper. "I'm a prisoner. Please help me."

I hear him laugh, as he pulls himself up off my bed, and feel his warmth behind my back as he grabs a few loose strands of hair and moves them over my shoulder with the rest. He grips the tiny zipper and tugs it down. The dress loosens as I hold up the sides. His fingers linger on my exposed back before he quickly withdraws them.

"Freedom is yours again."

"Thank you." I walk to the bathroom and close the door. I'm still tingling where he touched me as I shimmy out of the dress and get into the shower. I let the hot water wash over my tired body.

Ryan is flipping through channels by the time I walk out again. "Are you feeling better?" He gestures in my direction.

I nod and climb on to the bed next to him. It feels like the most natural thing in the world. Two friends flipping through channels together. "Anything on TV?"

"I've found a good movie for us to watch." He plays *Charlotte's Web*. "Is this an okay choice?"

I start bawling and cover my face with my hands. Ryan jumps up. He runs into my bathroom, and unable to find any tissues, he grabs a roll of toilet paper. As I wipe my eyes, my dad comes through the door with a tray.

"We brought some soup for supper," Suzie announces, then she sees the toilet roll in my hand and humor dances behind her eyes. "And I'll get a box of tissues too."

Ryan turns to my dad. "I am sorry, Jack. All I did was put a movie on and she broke down." He gestures towards my crying figure.

"It's okay. She will be fine in a day or two. You will see." Then he places a kiss on my head and gives the Prince a pat on the back. "I made the guest bed up for you, Ryan."

Suzie hands the tissues to Ryan, who quickly turns off the TV. I wipe my eyes and blow my nose. "I'm sorry, Ryan. You can drive home if you want."

"I am sorry you have had a rough day, Ann." He opens his arms for me to hug him a few moments after my dad and Suzie have exited the room.

I snuggle up and rest my head on his shoulder. "I know your day has been awful too. Thank you for being here for me."

"That is what friends are for." He pulls away and hands me my soup. "Now eat, my friend."

It smells amazing. I sip at the bowl and swirl the spoon around the red liquid. Tomato soup is one of my favorites and it's still hot.

I wake up the next morning on top of the covers with my head resting on Ryan's slow-moving chest. I rub my eyes as I look around. Recalling the events of the previous day, I move closer to the warmth of his chest. Ryan hums and places a hand on my back. It's comforting and I drift back to sleep.

In my nightmare, the end of the axe is coming down on Pecker. But before it falls, my head is in its path and Christian is gripping the other end. The self-righteous look on his face never leaves, as the blade slices through my neck and blue feathers fly high into the heavens.

Helping

I look in the mirror and groan. It's too bad Karen isn't here because her stomach muscles would be on fire. I find a comfortable pair of jeans and one of my favorite shirts that says *Mother Cluckers* on it. Even if my dad hates it, I know Ryan will enjoy its flawed humor.

The silence in the house is deafening. I make it to the kitchen and get my coffee started. Looking out the window, I smile at the chickens running around the yard. The coffee machine beeps, and I grab my chicken mug, blow on the contents, inhale the wonderful smell, and take a sip.

I sit on the bar stool and open the newspaper. I go to take another sip of coffee, as the back door opens. Ryan walks in and I spit out my coffee and chuckle. Ryan is shirtless, wearing overalls, boots, and a straw hat and he's followed in by my dad. "Have you two been busy?" I smirk.

Dad flicks the coffee machine back on. "Since someone overslept, Ryan volunteered to help around the farm." Even if he's trying to make me feel bad for sleeping in, his tone tells me he's pleased to have another man around the house. My dad kisses my head.

Ryan takes off my dad's old boots and straw hat and washes his hands. Those suits at the Palace hide a lot. His arm muscles ripple with the motion, and I force myself to look away. "It's not as easy as it looks, is it, Prince Ryan?"

He laughs a deep laugh. "Your dad could outrun and out lift me any day. I am exhausted. Did you sleep well?"

"Yes, better than I have in a while. It's good to be home."

Ryan stares out the window. "It's so peaceful here. I don't feel as though I have someone looking over my shoulder every second of the day." He turns and leans back. "Ann, I caught the news with your dad this morning and it seems those reporters, well, they had some interesting things to say about us."

"Fine, whatever. I really don't care anymore. Let them talk."

"My mom called me, asking if you reached out to the contractor yet."

With the trauma of Pecker's death, I forgot all about it. I grab the phone as Ryan reads me the number. The contractor picks up and we discuss a starting date. I see Ryan's dark eyes watching me. I make sure nothing is on my shirt. "What is it, cowboy?"

"Hey, laugh if you want, but I have never felt so comfortable." Then he flexes his tan bicep. "I feel so free."

"Oh, get a room you two." I gesture to him and his muscle.

"You handle yourself well on the phone. Is there anything you can't do?"

I wrap my palms around my mug. "There are plenty of things I can't do, Ryan."

"Really, like what?"

I talk into my coffee. "Like hold a relationship."

"That makes two of us. I am just a spoiled little Prince. Born and raised to step into my brother's shadow. The second choice for a leader one day. They made sure they had one — and a spare."

"That isn't true. You love photography and you are incredibly good at it. Plus, you are becoming a great farmer." I throw a dish towel at him.

He catches it and we share a moment of appreciation as we stare into each other's eyes. His phone rings in his pocket, and he breaks our connection to answer it before he passes the device to me. "Ann, it is for you."

"Ann, dear, how are you doing?" the Queen asks gently.

"After a good night's rest, I am feeling much better. Thank you for asking. I called the contractor today and he should be in by the end of the week to get started."

"That is great news, Ann. Do you plan on returning to the Palace by then?"

"Yes, I can leave as early as tonight if needed."

Ryan mouths, "No," at me from across the room.

"Great, but no rush, dear. I know you are going through a lot. Plus, after that news report this morning, you should lie low."

"Oh, really? I haven't seen it yet."

There is a long silence. "Oh, well, it's probably for the best. I will see you when you return. Please give Ryan my love." And she hangs up quickly.

"Your mom sends her love and she mentioned it was a good idea that I don't see the news report. Was it that bad?" He averts his eyes and rubs the back of his neck. "Ryan, just give me a rundown of the important details."

"It was reported that we left the Palace to be together."

"Excuse me?"

"The reporters took pictures of us hugging and walking back into your house after Pecker. They said you were heartbroken that Christian chose Mary and I was heartbroken about Cherie leaving me. It's been suggested that we were finding comfort in each other. Ann, I am sorry. I know it is a lot to take in."

"But surely Christian or your mom corrected them? I mean, it's lies. And we are being hurt because of it."

"Actually, no. Nobody corrected the reporters."

I jump off my bar stool, making it crash to the floor. "So what? They want us to look like lovestruck idiots. While they keep up their perfect image with the public. How is that fair?"

Ryan mutters, "It happens more than you realize. They need to show strength and unity. No matter who's hurt in their path to achieving it."

I've only had to deal with this for a short time, but Ryan has had to endure this his entire life. And even if I don't agree with it, being mad at him isn't going to help. "You're right. I didn't realize. But it doesn't justify their actions." I fix the bar stool and sit next to him. "There's nothing we can do about it now, so let's forget it. Does spaghetti sound good?"

"I haven't had spaghetti since I was little. It sounds great." Ryan rubs the back of his neck. "Before we start cooking, can I show you something outside?"

"A change of scenery is exactly what I need right now. Let me go throw on my boots real fast."

When we exit the little farmhouse a few minutes later, the sun is high, making my eyes water when I look up. Ryan throws his straw hat over my head and pulls the rim to my nose. I swat him away and lift the rim to see his eyes glittering down at me. I can't help but smile at his childish grin. He looks happy and carefree, walking around in the tall grass leading to my family headstones, located at the back of our property. I shove my hands in my pockets. I hate visiting this place because it reminds me of what has been taken from me.

Ryan stops at a fresh mound of dirt with a large boulder on top of it. When he kneels, he wipes the boulder, scaring a Monarch butterfly. I watch as it flutters skyward and towards our pear trees. "I know it isn't much, but I thought Pecker should have a memorial."

I kneel beside him as my eyes drop to the boulder. He wrote her name against the backdrop of a sunset. The painting must have taken him hours. My lip trembles and I place my hand on the stone memorial. The rough surface doesn't reflect the emotions swelling in my heart. "You painted this for her?"

"It wasn't just me. It was a team effort. Suzie brought over the art materials I needed, and your dad helped me find a good size rock. Oh, and I almost forgot. We gathered up some of her feathers and made you this. That way you'll always have her nearby." Ryan reaches into his pocket, pulls out a small clear jar, and hands it to me. I shake it softly and watch Pecker's feathers float around inside. I clutch the trinket to my chest. "I'm going to collect the eggs and bring them inside for your dad." Ryan squeezes my hand. "I'll see you back at the house."

I hear the grass crunch as he walks towards the henhouse. When I look up again, the tears are blurring my vision and a halo circles the top of his head. I place my forehead on the cold boulder as sobs rack my body.

Later that evening as I'm grabbing ingredients from the cupboard, I can feel the weight of Ryan's eyes on me. "Why don't you help me, cowboy?" I throw over my shoulder.

"But I did all the chores."

"I can teach you how to boil water, Prince Ryan. Come on." We start the water and sauce. "So, what were you and my dad talking about?"

He shrugs as he stirs the pasta. "We worked mostly, and he taught me about the farm and chickens. I feel like both my brain and my muscles are achy."

"I know what you mean. All the training to prepare me for the Palace life was mind-numbing." I drain the pasta and hand a strand to Ryan.

"Do you think it's done?" He tosses the stray noodle and it hits my hair.

"Ryan, what was that?" I grab and throw one, and it lands on his forehead.

"I meant to throw it at the wall, but I missed." He grins.

"Do you know how hard it will be to rinse that out of my hair?"

We laugh as we toss spaghetti at each other, unaware of my dad's watchful eyes. When he clears his throat, we both stop mid-throw. "What in the devil is going on in here? You two need to stop playing around and wasting food. Clean this up immediately."

I toss a piece of spaghetti at my dad's departing back and it sticks to his black t-shirt. We burst out laughing at the lone noodle survivor. I look around at the mess and step back to grab a sponge. I lose my footing on the slick floor. Ryan tries to catch me, but we both land with a thud, laughing as we go. I grab a noodle that is draped over his forehead and almost poking him in the eye. The second my fingers touch him, he stops laughing and blinks up at me. My heart quickens.

Then he smiles and leans his head back with a groan. "Ann, you are crushing me."

I swat him and roll off. "You started this."

"What? You asked me to test the noodle to see if it was done. Haven't you ever thrown it on the wall to test it?"

"Never, we *poor folk* eat it."

"Well, maybe you should wear it more often. I love your new hairstyle." Ryan runs a hand through my locks and past the noodle with a grin. I roll my eyes and shove a towel into his chest, making him push out a burst of air. We clean up the kitchen together and make plates for everyone. Suzie finds the noodle on my dad's back and they laugh. I join in until my stomach hurts and my gaze drops to Ryan's full plate.

"Ryan, are you not hungry?"

"I'm sorry, I'm feeling a little tired."

Dad rubs his stubble. "It is still early. But if we've worn you out, son, the guest room is made up if you want to rest."

"Why don't you shower, Ryan? I will clean up. And dad can find you some pajamas to borrow." I knock on the bathroom door several minutes later. "Ryan, are you feeling any better?"

His reply is muffled. "Just feeling a little under the weather. Maybe I have the flu."

I'd hate to worry the Queen, but a sick Prince is probably not the same as a sick commoner. "Ryan, I am going to call your mom and let her know we won't be coming back tonight." I can hear him groan.

"Do you have to?" Ryan opens the bathroom door to finish the conversation. He is towering over me with only a towel wrapped around his waist. I blush and turn away. I feel the steam from the shower radiating off his sculpted chest.

Luckily, Dad comes and hands Ryan some clothes. The Prince whines, "I don't want to worry my mom, Ann."

I run a palm across his forehead and hand him the phone. "I will drive you home or to the local doctor. Whatever you want. Just please call her." I keep my eyes on him as he walks into the guest room and plops down on the bed. I listen as he talks to the Queen and rub a hand up and down his back soothingly like my mom used to do when I had a fever.

He hangs up and places the phone on the nightstand. "She assumes it is a twenty-four-hour bug. She would feel better if I came home to get checked out."

"Well, I am sure she is worried about you. Do you want me to drive you?"

"Hmmm," he answers, as he drifts off to sleep. I stop rubbing his back. Instead of waking him, I slip out of his room to call his mom.

She answers quickly. "Ryan?"

"Sorry, Queen Elizabeth, it's me—Ann. Ryan just fell asleep, but he told me you wanted him to come home. Do you want me to drive him after he wakes up?"

She is quiet for a second. "How bad is he, Ann?"

"He is pale and hot with a fever. It came on all of a sudden while we were eating." I bite my fingernails. "He took a shower and a pain reliever. Maybe he will feel better with some sleep?"

"Would it be okay if I send a doctor over to check on him?"

"Of course, I will sit with him until the doctor arrives. Please feel free to call if you want to check up on him before then. I'll have the phone right beside me."

She breathes a sigh of relief. "Thank you, Ann. I will be in touch soon."

I tell my dad that the doctor is on his way and put a cold, wet washrag on Ryan's forehead to ease the fever. I lie next to him and blot his head while he sleeps. I run my fingers through his dark locks. Ryan groans and brings a hot hand to my face. "Thank you." And he drifts back to sleep.

The doctor wakes Ryan gently. I rub my eyes, confused, and slip off the bed. Ryan is still feverish and now his stomach hurts. Dad and Suzie stand next to me in the hallway. Suzie hands me some water and I sip it as we wait for the doctor to finish up.

I peek my head inside the room and the doctor waves me in as he returns his stuff to his bag. "He may have appendicitis. It is hard to tell for sure, so I am going to send him to the hospital to get some tests done. But he is being stubborn and refuses to go." He smiles at me. "I think you may have more luck with him. I will be waiting in the hall. I need to call the Queen with an update."

Ryan's eyes flutter open. "Don't you start too. I am fine. I just need this bug to run its course."

"Then why not get checked out?"

"I am having a good time here. I do not want to go back."

"Ryan, you know this place isn't going anywhere. You can visit anytime."

Dad walks in. "We just want to make sure you are okay."

"Fine, I will go get checked out. But I am looking forward to telling everyone I told you so." Ryan turns to me. "Ann? Are you coming home with me?"

Christian will be there with Lady Mary, and I'm not sure how I feel about that. Especially after all the rumors he started about me and Ryan. "Is that what you want me to do?"

"Yes. Then I can tell you I told you so in person."

"You'd better not, or I will tell your mother you threw spaghetti at me." After packing a few essentials, I meet Dad and the doctor by the car with Ryan already loaded inside. "Should I drive Ryan's car back?"

The doctor is the first to answer. "I think he would enjoy your company on the way." Then he slips inside.

I give my dad a tight hug. "Ryan will be fine, Ann," he says softly against my hair.

"I am afraid, Dad. Afraid I will lose him like I lost Mom." My eyes tear up.

"Ann, honey, do not be afraid to lose someone. Love them for as long as you can. Relish the time you have together."

Sick

The drive is long, as Ryan's stomach pain intensifies. By the time we get to the Palace, he is coated in sweat and is rushed to the hospital wing.

Standing in the hallway watching them push him away, I bite my fingernails. The doctor tells me that I can wait while they run tests. I drop my bag and sit on one of the hard, plastic chairs. My leg bounces up and down. I loathe hospitals. The smell, the equipment, and the uncertainty. I jump up as the Queen walks in.

"Thank you for convincing Ryan to come home and get checked out. The doctors are taking him into surgery now."

My face pales. "What? Why does he need surgery?"

"They need to remove his appendix, but the doctors are confident that he will make a full recovery."

"Ryan never would have left in the first place if it wasn't for me. I cause nothing but trouble." I pace the small area as my mind conjures images of my mom in her hospital bed. She was so thin and pale. Is that going to be Ryan? Does the universe hate me that much? My hand goes up to my scalp and I tug at my hair. The pain pulls me back to the present.

"Lady Ann, you couldn't have predicted this. It's not your fault." The Queen rubs my arm reassuringly.

Christian bursts in. He's disheveled and his hair is a disaster. "What are you doing here?" When his icy eyes pierce mine, I know I'm in trouble.

I step back and swallow. He has never looked this enraged before. I square my shoulders, pushing down my insecurities. "Ryan didn't want to travel alone in his condition."

"Ryan wouldn't be in surgery right now if he didn't go off gallivanting with you. This is all your fault."

"As much as you would like to, you can't blame everything on me, Prince Christian."

"My father's right. You've caused this family nothing but trouble." Christian's eyes bulge out of his head while his words spill out in a rush.

I rub my temples and take in a breath. I know I should be the bigger person, but I'm at my limit. "I'm glad Ryan isn't around to witness your toddler-sized tantrum. And with the way you are talking to me, he'd be embarrassed to have you as his brother. You need to man up and act your age. You are our future King for goodness' sake!"

He closes the gap between us in two quick strides and throws me against the wall. Christian wraps a hand around my neck. I try to pull his arm away but his hold is too strong. Adrenaline courses through my veins as I bring up a knee and send it into his groin as hard as I can. When he loosens his grip, I punch him in the nose and push him aside. Without his hand holding me up any longer, I collapse to the floor, gasping for air. My neck, throat, and lungs burn as I lean my head against the wall.

The Queen rushes over to me. "Ann! Are you okay? I am so sorry. I don't know what got into him. He has never behaved like this before." She offers me some water and sits beside me. Christian is going to be the death of me, literally. I get up and sit in the chair, feeling dizzy, and the Queen frowns and sets the water nearby. "Ann, I am going to ask a nurse to look you over. Then I need to check on Christian and find out what happened." She pats my leg and walks out of the room, leaving me alone and trembling.

A nurse comes in and offers ice to help with the swelling and bruising. My throat burns but the water chills it going down and I rest my head in my hands to cry. The door opens and I quickly straighten, fearing it's Christian coming back. My heart rate slows and evens out as Mary enters and closes the door behind her.

She sits down and turns to me. "Lady Ann."

"Princess Mary, or is that title reserved for after the wedding?"

"I suppose after we get married." She softens her voice. "Lady Ann, Prince Christian is going through a lot right now. I hope you know he did not mean to hurt you."

"So he sent you in here to apologize for him? He is a pathetic excuse for a human being." I turn to her. "Are you sure you won't be next?"

Mary pales. "He really is sorry."

"He can be sorry until he is blue in the face. Once I am done with this project, I will never have to see him again."

"Surely you aren't that naïve, Lady Ann. Even if you pretend you have no feelings for Prince Christian, what about Prince Ryan? You can't say you will never see him again."

I rub my sore neck. "I guess I cannot guarantee our paths won't cross. One day, Christian will be my King and he will be even harder to avoid." After a few minutes pass, I can't stand the uncomfortable quiet between us. When I met her, we were new to the competition and excited together. We were friends, until we were pitted against each other as rival love interests. And now we are no better than enemies. I grope around my mind for something to say to ease the tension. "I wonder what is taking so long."

I poke my head out. Vinny is with another guard outside the door. I feel better knowing that Christian can't get to me. "Lady Ann."

"Are you here for my protection—or his?"

He smirks. "Both."

"Can I get some food and see Karen? I could really use a friendly face right now."

On the way to the kitchen, I run into Christian and his mom talking. I freeze like a deer in headlights, and Vinny touches the small of my back. Christian's eyes soften as he watches me. He opens his mouth to say something but thinks better of it and walks away. The Queen makes her way over to me. Her eyes assess the damage on my neck. "How are you feeling, Lady Ann?"

"I'm feeling better. I just came out to get some air. How are you doing? Is there any word on Ryan yet?"

"I am holding it together for now. There is no update on Ryan. I told Christian to keep his distance from you, and although he is sorry, he doesn't want to be apart from his brother, under the circumstances."

"Christian should be the one with Ryan. I'll get out of the way and stay with Karen for now."

"That's considerate of you. Thank you for understanding, Lady Ann." She unexpectedly collects me in a hug. I return it gently. "Try not to worry, dear. Ryan is strong. I will contact Vinny when we have more information on Ryan's condition."

I make a few sandwiches, grab some chips and sodas, and go to Karen's room. She hugs me tight, then embraces Vinny. "Ann. What a wonderful surprise. What are you doing back so soon?"

"It is a long story."

"What the heck happened to your neck?"

I hand her a sandwich and we catch up on everything.

"I hope Prince Ryan feels better soon. I am sure with all the experts working on him, he will be on his own two feet shortly. I can't believe Prince Christian did that to you. I really hope the punishment fits the crime. I would love to wrap my hands around his neck and squeeze some sense into that privileged brat."

"Well, on the bright side, I get to hang out with you and Vinny while we wait for the outcomes."

Karen extends her left hand, and the ring on her finger catches the light.

"Oh, my goodness. Congratulations. I'm so happy for you two." I quirk a brow. "It is Vinny, right?"

"Of course, it's Vinny. Who else would it be?"

"Well, it's so sudden I wasn't sure." I hug them both and try to keep the smile on my face as I sit back on the bed and watch them interact. They talk about how Vinny got on one knee and proposed by a beautiful lake house just outside the city. And how he did it right as the sun was going down.

"What are you thinking about over there, Ann? You look like you are miles away."

"Do you think Ryan is a good guy?"

"Well, of course he is, or you wouldn't be with him."

I blush. "The news is all lies. I'm not with him. We are just friends."

"Really? And that's all? That looks like an awful lot of worry on your face for just a friend."

"Yes, we are both getting out of relationships, though mine never really got going properly, but it's complicated."

"Every relationship is complicated, Ann. You two need to stop dancing around each other and make a move already."

I laugh and shake my head. "I guess I'm afraid."

"What are you afraid of, Ann?"

"I'm afraid he's going to be like Christian."

"Aw, sweetie. They are two very different people."

"I'm going to shower and try to cover this up with some makeup." I touch my bruised neck. I take a long shower, attempting to wash the day down the drain while thinking about what Karen said. When I'm done, I dress and see Karen and Vinny hugging and enjoying each other's company.

She turns to me and gets up to grab my makeup. "Sit," she commands as she dabs my sore neck.

"Did everybody believe that news report about Ryan and me?"

"I think so. I mean, you two always seemed close and comfortable with each other while you were here."

"So, everyone thinks we are a couple?"

She nods and finishes the touch-up on my bruise. "Well, that's as good as it is going to get."

"Thank you for your help. I have never been great with makeup or covering things up. I hate lying." To keep my hands busy, I pull out a deck of cards from my bag. "Do you want to play a game to pass the time?"

We go to the servants' breakroom and play rummy at a table. Karen smiles at Vinny. "So, what time do you get off babysitting duty?"

"Hey!" I protest.

She sticks her tongue out at my pout.

"Until I'm instructed otherwise. Trust me, it's more like bodyguard duty, Karen. You should have seen Prince

Christian. I will gladly keep watch, so it doesn't happen again."

"I am sorry that happened to you, Ann. It's awful. Hopefully, he learns his lesson."

"I hope so too." Vinny nods as he sips his coffee, then responds to a call in his earpiece. "Copy that. On our way." He straightens his uniform while looking at me. "Prince Ryan is out of surgery and asking for you."

My heart skips a beat and I stand quickly. I stumble over my feet as I start to clean the table.

Karen places a comforting hand on my trembling one. "I can clear up, Ann. You two go and see your Prince."

Surprises

We arrive at Ryan's hospital room, and Vinny knocks on the door. The Queen answers and ushers us inside. Ryan is pale and out of it still, but he's better than when I last saw him. I wring my hands as I stand at the edge of the bed.

He opens his arms wide for me. "There she is." And he holds me in a tight hug. "I was wondering where you went. I thought you would not leave my side," he says playfully.

"Did you expect me to hold the scalpel for the doctor too?" I swipe at my eyes.

He runs a hand through my hair. "I miss the spaghetti highlights." He brushes my bruised neck and I flinch. "What on earth is that?"

I turn to the Queen, unsure how to respond.

Ryan glares at me. "Ann. What happened?"

I shake my head, unable to answer him. The Queen places a reassuring hand on my arm and walks to Ryan. "Now, Ryan, you need to calm down, sweetie."

"Does this have something to do with my brother? You are covering for him, aren't you, Mother?"

"It was a misunderstanding, an accident. He was worried about you and under a lot of pressure."

Ryan slams his balled-up fist on his side table. "Stop it. Just get out."

She backs up towards the door, watching him with wary eyes. "Ryan?"

"Now." We both turn to leave. "Ann, stay," he commands.

I cautiously walk over and sit down beside him. I've never been afraid of a man in my life. I've never had reason to be, but after the attack, I'm terrified and Ryan is so angry. I've never seen him like this before. He reaches over and I flinch before his hand can touch mine. He holds me gently and pulls me over to him. I squeeze beside him on the small hospital bed. I rest my head on his chest, listening to his heartbeat.

"I would never hurt you—never. Please say that you believe that. You have nothing to be afraid of when you're with me. I know you're upset about what happened, but you are safe now. Please tell me what happened. I need to know."

I recount the details as best I can and feel him stiffen.

"I am sorry this happened to you, Ann. He has an anger problem, but it has never turned into a physical confrontation. He needs help. Or a good old-fashioned butt-kicking, and you better believe I'll be the first in line to give it to him. He will never lay a finger on you again. You have my word."

"You mustn't go after him, Ryan. You are so much better than that. He is your brother and, unfortunately, our future King."

"You always have more faith in me than anyone else." And he whispers, very faintly before he drifts off to sleep with me in his arms, "And that is why I love you."

I try to pull back, but he is sleeping, and his arm is trapping me. "Ryan?"

"Hmm?"

"Did you say you loved me?"

"Mmmhmmm."

I groan at the lack of a coherent response. I turn to Vinny, who's quietly watching us from the corner, and he gives me a thumbs up. I shake my head and snuggle into Ryan's body, being careful not to touch the oversized bandage on his stomach.

I wake up to the sound of voices and bright lights. There's a doctor and a nurse in the room with us. I jump off the bed and Ryan laughs behind me. "Good morning, sleepyhead."

I blush and move out of their way as they check his stitches and vitals. Vinny has been replaced by another guard and must be off duty at last. I smile, realizing how tired he must be, and I'm glad he's finally able to get some rest.

"What are you thinking about over there?" Ryan brings me back to the present.

"How happy Karen must be with her new fiancé. And how nice it must be to have a normal relationship."

The doctor finishes looking him over and reports, "Everything looks good. You can be moved to your own room whenever you are ready. We will have a wheelchair for you and your room is set up for your recovery."

I watch them leave and turn back to Ryan, who's avoiding making eye contact with me. "Aren't you happy to be going back to your room, Ryan?"

"I wish I could give you the normal relationship you want."

"It's not in my cards to have a normal life. But when you had to have your operation, you scared the life out of me. It made me realize that I would like a relationship with you, normal or not."

He smiles brightly and pulls me into a hug as his door opens and the Queen pops her head in. He waves her forward. "Did the doctors update you, Mom?"

"Yes, dear, they did. How are you feeling?"

"Good." He looks to me. "Better."

I give them some privacy to talk and leave with the guard in tow. As I walk to the small waiting area, I see Mary and Christian holding hands and sitting together. I freeze as my eyes meet Christian's and he jumps up. His hair is a mess, his clothes are wrinkled, and he looks like he hasn't slept in days. "Ann, please wait. I am sorry."

"Don't come near me." I can barely stand to speak to him, and I'm terrified to have him anywhere near me. "You can see Ryan if you want. I am going to get some coffee."

"I know it is no excuse, but I was scared, and I blamed you for what happened when I shouldn't have. I didn't want to lose him. I know you, of all people, can empathize with that. Can you ever forgive me?"

"I will try," I push out slowly.

The early-morning sun is shining through the stained-glass windows of the break room, creating light prisms on the floor. I feel optimistic. Ryan is healing, and soon I will be back working and staying busy. I make two cups of coffee and take one to Karen to surprise her. I knock lightly and open the door.

"Karen? I know it is your day off and you hate waking up early. But I brought you something hot and black." I tell the guard to wait outside and see two bodies in the bed. I stop and blink. Do I have the right room? I glance behind me at the door to confirm my location. "Vinny, is that you?"

He waves at me.

My face turns red and I turn to Karen. "Karen? What's going on?"

"We eloped! Now where is my coffee?"

"Why would you elope?" I stammer.

She shrugs as she reaches out, grabs her mug, and sips. "After Ryan's health scare, we realized life is too short to wait any longer." She recites the story of their adventure at a small chapel in the city.

Vinny stretches, sits up, and steals Karen's coffee. He kisses her and says, "Time for guard duty." Then with a wink towards me, he walks out to change for work.

Karen tilts her head at my silence. "A penny for your thoughts?"

"I was wondering about my own future."

We change our clothes as we talk about boys and I congratulate her. I update her about Ryan and Christian, and she tells me how wonderful her first night was as Vinny's wife. As we walk, Karen whispers, "Has the King visited Ryan?"

"Not that I know of, but I haven't been around the whole time. Plus, I am sure he has other things he has to worry about."

"I don't know. He seemed really mad when Ryan left with you. And now this happens."

As we get to the hospital wing, I hear Karen giggle. Vinny pinches her as he passes to relieve my guard. Mary and the Queen are sitting in the waiting area. "They are getting Ryan ready to move now. He is excited to be in his own room again," Queen Elizabeth explains.

Christian appears through the doors, pushing Ryan in a wheelchair. They are both laughing, and I'm shocked that they made up so fast but I'm glad to see them happy. They stop in front of us and Ryan locks eyes with me and smiles. "Ann, would you mind pushing me to the elevator?" Ryan asks.

I remember hobbling around on my crutches and using the stairs. I glare at Christian. "You have an elevator?"

He laughs. "I'm sorry. I thought it was funny at the time." He has the grace to look sheepish for once. Maybe it's time to let bygones be bygones. But as long as I live, I'll never trust Christian again and will avoid ever having to be alone with him.

"Of course, I can push you, Ryan. Just tell me where to go."

The Queen smiles at Vinny and says, "Thank you, Vinny. Ann does not require a guard at the moment."

Ryan clears his throat. "Ann, I know what Christian did is unacceptable and nothing will ever excuse his behavior."

I scoff as I put one foot in front of the other. "That is the understatement of the century."

"I agree. But Christian did start anger management counseling. He is working towards improving himself."

"He has a long road ahead of him, Ryan."

"Ann, I will always protect you from him. But please understand that Christian is my brother, and I will also always love him and be there when he needs me."

"It will take time but I will try to forgive him."

He pushes the elevator button and we rise to the third floor. "Thank you, Ann." Ryan reaches back and squeezes my hand.

Christian enters before I can settle Ryan into his room and I instinctively back away. "Ann, I am really sorry for my behavior."

"You keep telling me you're sorry, but you are always hurting me, Christian."

"Please, Ann, you don't understand."

"Then tell me. What is it that I don't understand?"

Ryan clears his throat. "Christian, could you please give us a minute?"

The Prince walks out, looking as though he's trying to control his temper.

"Ann, I will give you my word that my brother will never do that to you again."

I'm not sure if that is a promise he can keep. I want to trust Ryan, but I can't shake my unease. Then I frown, thinking about all the special attention he has been giving me since we have been back at the Palace. I pull away. "Ryan, are you pretending to be with me to keep up appearances?"

He gently runs a hand down my face and under my chin. Then he lowers his warm lips to mine. My eyes go wide at first, hesitant. Then I meet his kiss. It's unbelievably soft and tender. Exactly like him.

Realization

Ryan pulls away with a smile. "Ann, you never cease to amaze me."

"Are you trying to persuade me to stay?"

"Why? Is it working?"

"I think I may need more persuading." I grin and lean towards him and we embrace again. Christian returns a few moments later, and I slide off the bed to the floor. "I'm going to go. I will come back to check on you, Ryan."

"Ann, please wait. You don't have to leave. I will." Christian frowns.

"Don't be ridiculous. I'll go."

"You are the one being ridiculous," he says as he closes Ryan's door.

I stop at his words and he bangs into my back with an audible *oof.* I face him with my hands on my hips. Something shifts in his gaze and I see that smokey look I've come to recognize. I step away, putting distance between us.

"I love it when you get fired up." He moves his hand to my face. "Your cheeks get rosy and puffy."

"Christian, don't touch me."

We hear a voice behind us, calling out the Prince's name, and we jump out of our thoughts. The King is glaring at us. My face turns red and I take a step back. Christian stands in front of me. "Yes, Father?"

"Correct me if I am wrong, but you should be in the office, should you not?"

Christian leaves with a glance towards me as he goes.

"Lady Ann? Or is it just Ann? I am confused," the King asks, staring at me, his eyes unblinking.

I give a forced laugh. "I'm not entirely sure myself, my King. But as your word goes, I will accept whatever you deem appropriate."

"It's a beautiful day. Ann, let's go for a walk outside."

Christian stops at his father's words. "Dad, I think Mom needs your help with the financial report." I can hear the tension in his voice. Fear crawls up my spine.

"Trust me, son, I will be back soon enough. This will not take long." The King leads me into the garden where we can be alone. My palms are sweating. "Ann, we have a serious problem."

"Sorry, my King?"

"Both of my sons have feelings for you. I convinced Christian to make the right decision and change his mind."

"Don't you think that should have been his choice?" I squeak out.

"Not when it is the incorrect choice. He is this country's future and he needs a strong and obedient wife."

"Surely, my King, you must trust your son's judgment? Christian is intelligent, and completely capable of choosing what he wants in his future wife."

The King stops and looks down at me, his face obviously heated. "Are you questioning me and accusing me of not trusting my son?"

"Of course not, but…"

"No *buts*. I know best. Always. And it would be wise to remember that. I think it is time for you to go back home. Permanently. Where you belong."

"If I'm nothing and not a threat, then it shouldn't matter if I am here or at home, right?"

"How is your neck healing?"

I raise a hand to my throat as the King steps forward and closes the gap between us, pinning me to the Palace wall with his body.

He whispers in my ear with narrowed eyes. "Because as much as I do not like hurting women, I can make that bruise look like child's play."

I swallow and stand tall. "Why do you feel you have to bully everyone around you to get your way?"

He laughs and it's a wild sound. "Oh, Ann, I am not bullying. This is just a warning, my dear." He runs a hand under my chin. I cringe and try to pull back. "Stay away from my children. This is your one and *only* chance. I can make you disappear. Or maybe I should pay your father a visit first?" He releases my chin as suddenly as he grabbed it. "Do we understand each other?"

"Yes."

"Yes, what?"

"Yes, my King, I understand."

"Good girl, Ann. I hope you have a safe trip home." He walks back inside the Palace without a backwards glance.

When he has turned the corner and out of my view, I sink to the ground, taking deep breaths. I hear footsteps as Vinny approaches.

"Ann, are you okay?" He kneels next to me. "Prince Christian told me to stay close but hidden just in case."

"You knew the King was crazy?"

"No, but I wanted to keep an eye on you, especially if the Prince was worried."

I suck in air and tell him what happened between me and the King. "I feel like I am going to throw up, Vinny. The King hides it well, but that man is insane."

"Ann, you know I will do whatever I can to keep you safe. I can find some other guards willing to help too."

"Vinny, please, I can't have anyone else getting hurt because of me. I will do what he wants and leave. Do you think the Queen knows about this?"

"I don't think so. She is the kindest woman I know, and she has always been on your side. I have a feeling this has been hidden from her."

"It will be all right, Vinny. Don't do anything stupid. Remember, you have a wife to look after now."

"Yeah, she is pretty lucky, isn't she?" He attempts to lighten the mood.

"Vinny, could you please tell the Princes that I am safe and going back home. And that I... never mind. That's it." A silent tear slides down my cheek.

I flick my eyes to the ground, and when I look up again, I watch as a man with dark hair and green eyes walks over in jeans and a black collared shirt. He smiles at me as he comes closer. "Lady Ann?"

I try to remember where I have seen him before.

"I am the contractor, Dan, for the chicken coop. We spoke on the phone," he reminds me as if sensing my confusion.

I shake his hand. "I am sorry, sir, but I have been removed from the project. You will have to speak to the Queen."

His young, weather-worn face creases as he frowns. "Please, Lady Ann, I have men needing paychecks for their families. It should only take a few minutes and a signature. Then I can make my men happy and pay them to get started."

I know how hard these guys work and how difficult it is to find well-paying jobs. This could be my last good deed before I leave. "Okay, Mr. Dan, this way."

Vinny gently grabs my arm. "Ann, are you sure this is a good idea?"

I nod and wave him off as I show Dan around. We review the plans, he makes some adjustments, we shake hands, and I sign off for the work to officially start.

Dan beams. "Thank you, Lady Ann, this means a lot. It is nice to see a Lady around here who actually cares about the people."

"Thank you, Dan. Compassion is something I think we all need more of in this crazy, upside-down world." I look up into the sky and frown, as I observe the sun lowering and darkness rolling in. I was hoping to see the project through, but I trust the Queen and Dan to do a decent job with it.

Two Sides

I get the rest of my things before heading home, and Karen embraces me in a tight hug. "Ann, I was so worried when Vinny told me what happened to you. It seems Prince Christian isn't the only one who needs counseling around here. The King is out of his mind to threaten you like that."

"You are the closest thing to a sister I have, Karen. Please stay in contact and visit me often. Don't forget about me, or all the great times we had together."

Karen wipes my tear away with her thumb. "Ditto, sis."

"Vinny, have you come to get all weepy on me too?"

"Not me. I only came by to let you know I relayed your message to the Princes."

"Thank you for watching out for me. Make sure you do the same for Karen and my boys."

"I called for a car to take you home. It's waiting for you outside. Do you want us to walk you out?" Karen offers.

"No, it's easier to say goodbye here."

I embrace them each one more time, close the Palace door behind me, and slide into the car before we make our way down the long driveway. The man pulls over and turns off the car. My heart races as I look out the dark window but I don't see why we have stopped. I'm terrified that the King is coming for me. I crane my neck towards the driver and realize that it's Christian watching me in the rearview mirror.

"Christian, what are you doing?"

183

"I couldn't let you go without saying a proper goodbye. Ryan wouldn't hear of it."

I pale and look around outside. "But what about your dad?"

"I am sorry about him. I never thought it would get this far."

"So, it's true? He is the reason you chose Mary?"

He pivots to pass me a velvet box. "This has been in my pocket for some time now. I had it custom made, but since my father has forbidden me to marry you, you can keep it as a parting gift instead. To remember our adventures together, Ann, and to remind you what could have been if things were different."

I open the box and inside is a beautifully designed, gold and diamond engagement ring with a chicken in the center. My vision blurs from the tears forming. It's the most thoughtful gift I have ever received.

"That was the exact reaction I always imagined."

"Christian, it's perfect. But I cannot take this. You are marrying Mary and it would be inappropriate."

He smiles sadly and pushes the ring on my finger. "It is a perfect fit for the perfect lady." Then he sighs. "I am sorry you got mixed up in all this, Ann. I honestly didn't mean for you to get hurt. Please keep the ring. I want you to have it. You deserve that and so much more, and I am sorry I can't give it to you."

"And I would do it all over again, or some of it anyway—the good bits. What about Mary? Does she know about your dad?"

"She was hesitant about the engagement after she knew I was asking you. But Father took care of that. He scared her into submission by threatening to hurt her family if she left the Palace. It's not the best way to start a marriage but what can we do."

"And your mom?"

"She has no idea that my dad is the way that he is. And he would murder anyone who told her. She loves him and is blind to his ways. He keeps his threats and violence private and he has his own guards he uses when needed. The ones who are not afraid to get their hands dirty and keep it quiet."

There is a rap on Christian's window. We jump and a muscled guard gestures for Christian to wind it down.

"Good evening, Derek, how can I help you?"

The man smirks and my arm hairs stand on end and my blood runs cold. This must be one of the guards Christian was talking about and I bet he's not here to have a tea party. "Prince Christian, the King requests your immediate presence, please."

The Prince weighs his options, as if trying to figure out an escape route, before finally conceding. "Of course, Derek. And what about Lady Ann?"

"She is my responsibility. I will make sure she gets where she needs to go." Before Christian can protest, Derek opens his door and flashes a silver blade. "My Prince, I am ordered to take whatever measures I need to take. Please meet your father like a good little boy and leave Ann to me."

Christian's eyes flare in anger. I exit the car before the situation gets out of hand. Christian jumps out too. "Ann. Stop. You don't know what he is capable of."

Derek pushes Christian back into the car and grabs my wrist. He pulls me to him with the blade's edge pressed firmly against my back. "Go to your father, my Prince. We don't want any bloodshed, do we?" he purrs into my ear.

"Please go, Christian. I will be fine."

Vinny is approaching us with a hand on the gun in his side holster. He watches Derek. "Prince Christian, do you need my assistance?"

I attempt to yell out a warning to Vinny, but Derek clasps a hand over my mouth. "This is below your pay grade, soldier. Step down and return to your babysitting duty. This is official business from the King."

Before Vinny can draw his weapon, I see a flash of silver, and my friend falls to the ground, writhing in pain with the knife's hilt sticking out of his stomach and blood soaking through his blue uniform. Christian runs to him and applies pressure to the wound. I clamp my teeth down on Derek's hand and scream. I feel a sharp poke in my back, blood trickles down my spine, and I wince. My eyes are glued to Vinny and Christian on the ground as my energy seeps out of me and I stop fighting.

Derek points his knife at Christian. "This is your fault, boy. I warned you." Then the King's guard throws me over his shoulder and starts stalking back towards the Palace. I can't tell where we are going as the tears keep streaming. What will happen to Vinny? I cannot believe how fast this has escalated. My friend is hurt and I am at the guard's mercy.

Derek drops me on a canvas surface. I'm in a cell with bars on the window. It's cold and dark with a cot, a small toilet, and nothing else. I glare at my captor and pound my fists on his chest. "Why did you do this? Vinny didn't do anything to deserve being stabbed. You are a monster!"

Derek laughs as he shoves me away. "He got in my way and I have my orders." He draws his knife from his side and runs the blade across his fingertip. "Ann, you should be more worried about yourself. The King ordered you to leave. And yet, here you are. What were the two of you planning on doing? Eloping?"

"No, we weren't eloping. I was going home."

"How stupid do you think I am?" He pins me to the wall, running the blade along the bruise on my neck, and whispers close to my ear, "I am going to have fun with you later, sweet Ann. But first, I need to check in with the King and have your guard friend's accident erased." He returns his knife to his belt and leaves the cell, locking the door behind him. "Until later, my Lady." He bows and walks away, his manic laughter echoing against the bare walls.

Loose Ends

Time passes slowly as dread overcomes my other senses. I look at the engagement ring Christian gave me. I twist it in my fingers. There is an inscription: *to my hen.*

I lie on the cot and curl into a ball. I'm so exhausted I drift off into a dark sleep until I hear a door shut. I look around wildly in the dimly lit cell.

"Ann?" That voice sounds like Karen. Am I still dreaming?

"Karen? Is that you?" I jump up. "Karen. You need to get out of here before Derek comes back. The cell is locked, and unless you have the key, you can't help me. Get away before he catches you. But, first, please tell me... how is Vinny?"

"He is in the hospital wing. He is incredibly lucky Christian got him there in time. The doctors think he will make a full recovery. And do not worry about Derek."

I tilt my head in confusion.

"Listen, Ann, I cannot go into detail but just know you are safe, and everything will be better in the morning," she whispers through the bars.

"What? Karen, what do you mean?"

She tugs her hands away from the metal. "Have I ever let you down?"

"No, you haven't."

"And I do not plan on starting today either."

I hear her footsteps get softer and softer. I wait, hoping she will return, but nobody comes. I sit back on the cot and stare at the spot where she had been until I can't see anything but darkness.

Someone is shaking me and I wake, startled. As my vision focuses on the figure in front of me, I see a pair of icy eyes gazing down at me. "Oh, Ann, I thought I was going to lose you forever." He embraces me.

"Christian, what is happening? Where is Derek?"

"The King passed away in his sleep last night."

"What? How? Are you okay?"

He nods. "He was not a good man to be around, but he was my father. My mother is beside herself with grief. She found him this morning."

I pull back, shocked. "Wait. That means... you will be King."

He nods solemnly. "Let's get you out of here."

The Palace is in confusion. People are crying and wearing black. Christian opens Ryan's door and leads me inside. Ryan looks up from his bed with dark circles under his eyes, his hair ruffled, and I can't help but question who lost more sleep. Me or him?

I run to him and he hugs me. "Christian told me what happened. Did they hurt you?"

"I got off a lot easier than Vinny. I have a scratch and a few future nightmares. But I'll live."

He looks at his brother as he rubs my back. "Thank you."

Christian sits on the edge of the bed. "Things are going to get intense around here. Are you up for it?"

Ryan nods.

"A wedding and a funeral?" I ask.

"And a Coronation," Christian adds.

I stare at him and wonder how he feels about being King. No matter what happens, Ryan will have his back. Although the King is gone, I get the feeling the country will be in good hands in the coming years, between having Christian as their leader and Ryan as his ally.

I look down at Ryan's palm in mine, Christian's ring visible on my other hand, and wonder what my future holds. Will Christian pursue me again now that he can choose who he wants? Or will he step aside and allow his brother a chance at happiness?

Thank You

Thank you for reading my book! Could you leave a quick **review** on Amazon? Reviews are so important, and I would greatly appreciate it.

I hope you enjoyed Ann's first adventure and will continue to read what happens in her life. She is strong and has so much compassion to offer the world.

See Ann again, in all her feathered glory, as she continues her adventure in *Book 2: Plucked*, *Book 3: Molting*, and *Book 4: Split Feather*. Available NOW!

About the Author

Brittany Putzer was born and raised in Central Florida, so the need for sunshine (and coffee) is imbedded in her DNA.

Growing up, she turned to books to escape, because it was easier to pretend to be a wizard, vampire, or damsel in distress.

Her books are a wonderful blend of dark and light, with colorful sprinkles of sarcasm, twists and turns, sweet kisses and, on occasion, dramatic cliff-hangers...

She hopes her books can help readers remember how strong they really are... if only they keep moving and fighting the good fight.

Scan the QR code to chat with Brittany on social media, sign up for her exclusive newsletter, and look at her other romance books.

Additional Titles by the Author

Feathered Dreams Series (a rags-to-riches, clean romance):

Join Ann and be swept into a world of swoon-worthy characters, glittering gowns, and unrelenting intrigue.

Ann is beginning to see how naïve she has been, though by no fault of her own. Farming side by side with her father, away from the drama of the outside world, is what she has always loved most. But now that she is at the Palace, she is forced to focus on other people and their daily struggles. In the midst of her personal growth, she starts to realize how cruel the world can be. Will she shy away and run back to the familiarity of her old life? Or can she share her unique sense of compassion and fierce loyalty to help those in need?

Feathered Dreams (Book 1)

Plucked (Book 2)

Molting (Book 3)

Split Feather (Book 4)

To Be Titled (Book 5) TBA 2023

Wolves of Cold Creek (18+, paranormal romance):

The Cold Creek packs are loyal—while bursting with mouthwatering, unclaimed shifters—all just waiting for their mates. Why not drop in and enjoy the picturesque views by day and scorching fires at night? Don't be shy. They don't bite... hard.

Scarlett's Tail

Sky's Tail

Lily's Tail TBA

The General's Report TBA

Rebel's Revenge TBA

The Spellcaster TBA

Cooking Up Disaster (slow-burn romance):

Step into the Decadent Cup and grab something hot!

Blake has a tough exterior but a heart of gold. In the small town of Jasper, he owns the Decadent Cup café where he's selling handcrafted coffee, baking killer banana nut muffins, and staying the hell away from long-term relationships.

Amy's a struggling single mom with no time for love, because she had it with her deceased husband. When her best friend asks her for a favor, she jumps at the chance. But this change in events brews a challenging new blend of trouble, and she'll be cooking up a disaster with the town alpha.

Available now only on Kindle Vella.